Disney Fairies

# Tinker Bell

## *and a Far-Too-Secret Secret*

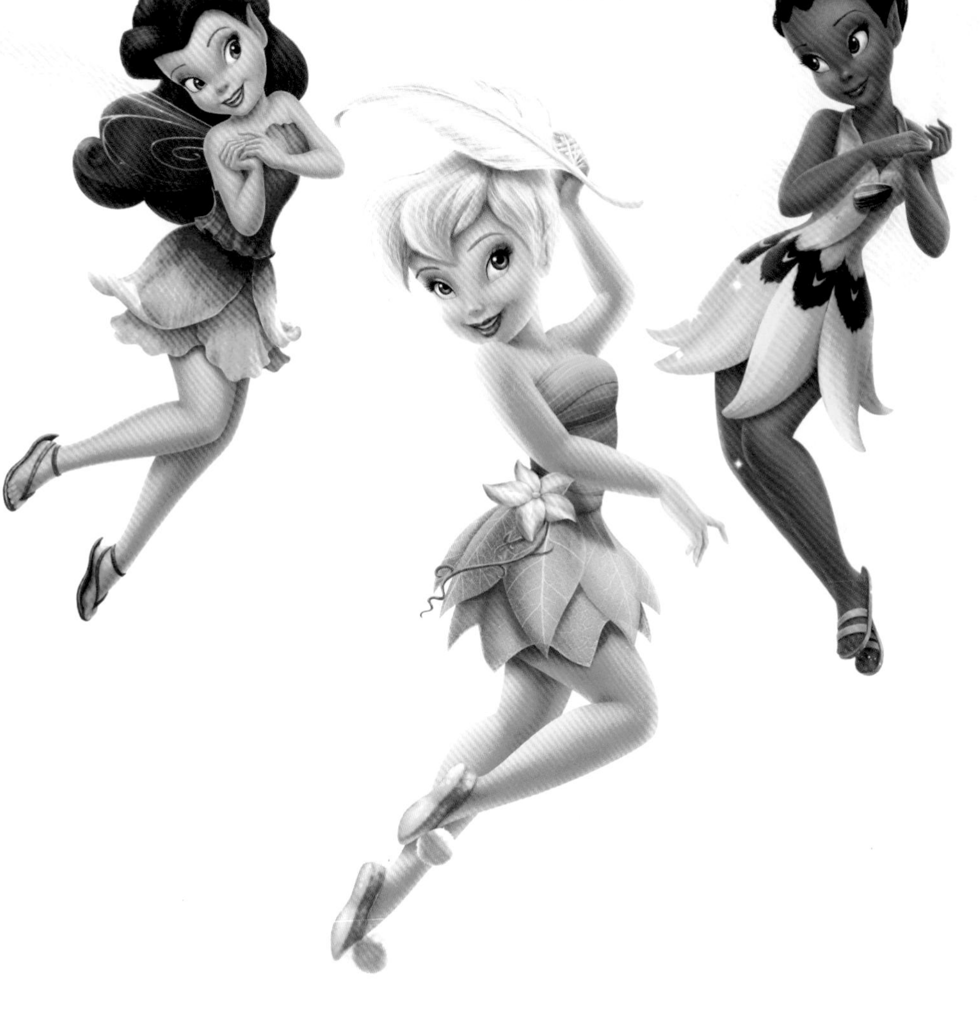

PAPERCUTZ™

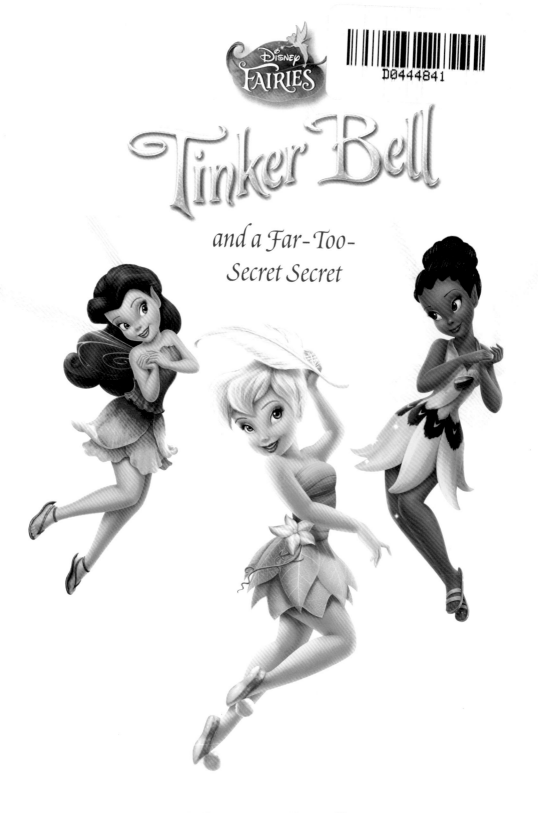

# Graphic Novels Available from PAPERCUTZ™

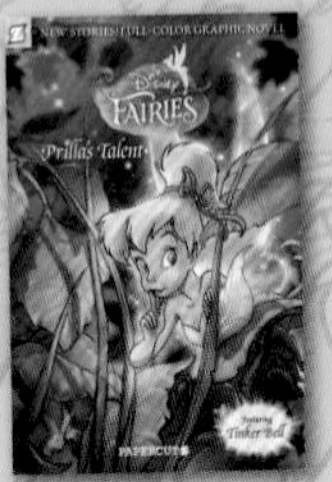

**Graphic Novel #1**
"Prilla's Talent"

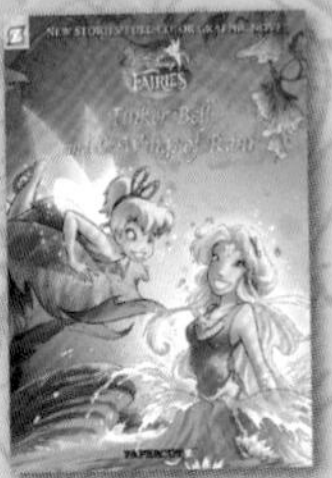

**Graphic Novel #2**
"Tinker Bell and the Wings of Rani"

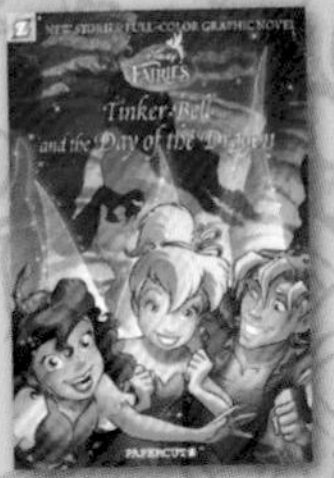

**Graphic Novel #3**
"Tinker Bell and the Day of the Dragon"

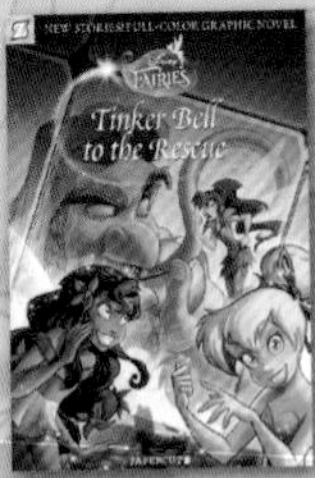

**Graphic Novel #4**
"Tinker Bell to the Rescue"

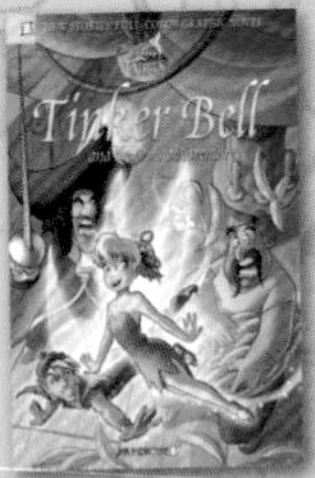

**Graphic Novel #5**
"Tinker Bell and the Pirate Adventure"

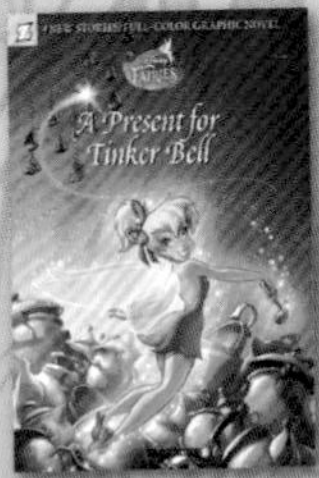

**Graphic Novel #6**
"A Present for Tinker Bell"

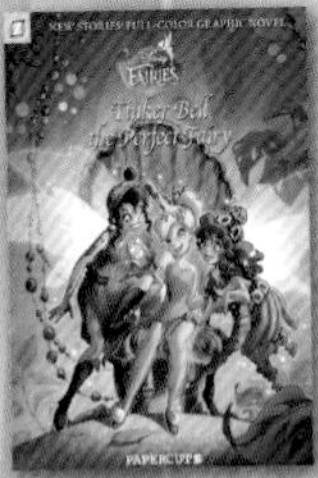

**Graphic Novel #7**
"Tinker Bell the Perfect Fairy"

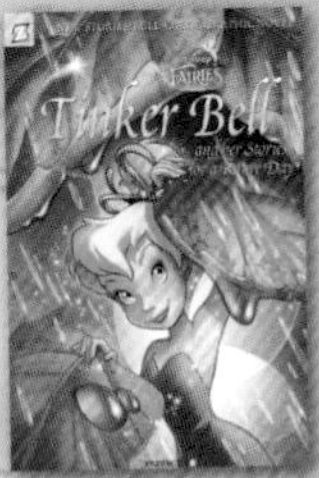

**Graphic Novel #8**
"Tinker Bell and her Stories for a Rainy Day"

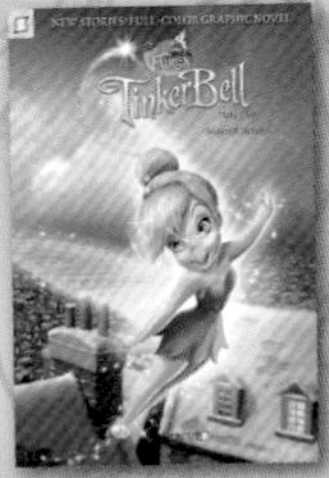

**Graphic Novel #9**
"Tinker Bell and her Magical Arrival"

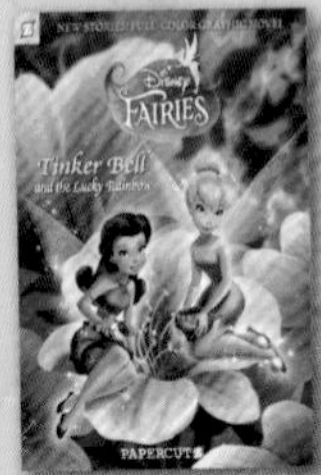

**Graphic Novel #10**
"Tinker Bell and the Lucky Rainbow"

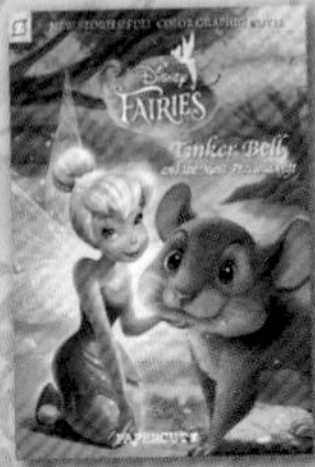

**Graphic Novel #11**
"Tinker Bell and the Most Precious Gift"

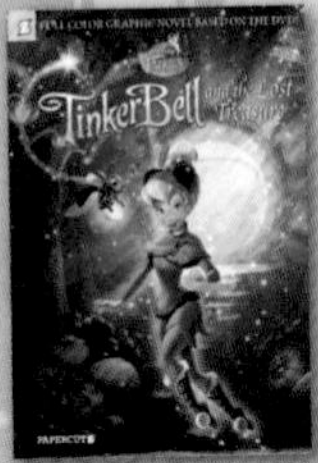

**Graphic Novel #12**
"Tinker Bell and the Lost Treasure"

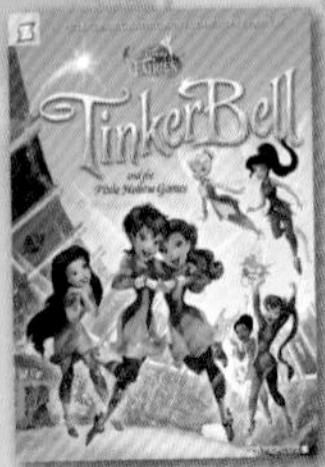

**Graphic Novel #13**
"Tinker Bell and the Pixie Hollow Games"

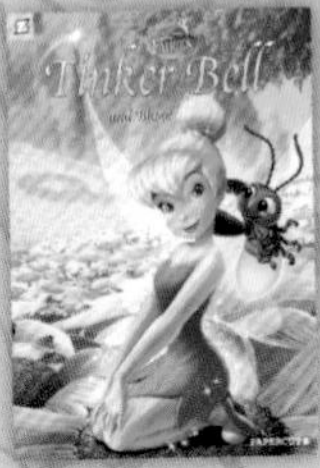

**Graphic Novel #14**
"Tinker Bell and Blaze"

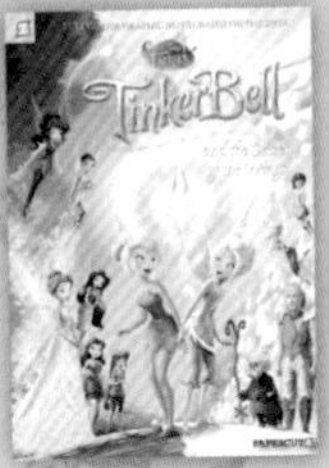

**Graphic Novel #15**
"Tinker Bell and the Secret of the Wings"

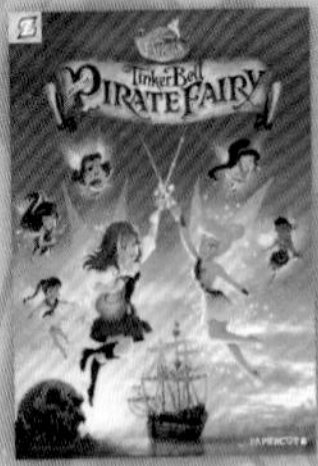

**Graphic Novel #16**
"Tinker Bell and the Pirate Fairy"

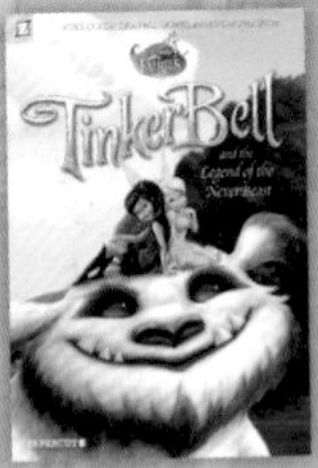

**Graphic Novel #17**
"Tinker Bell and the Legend of the NeverBeast"

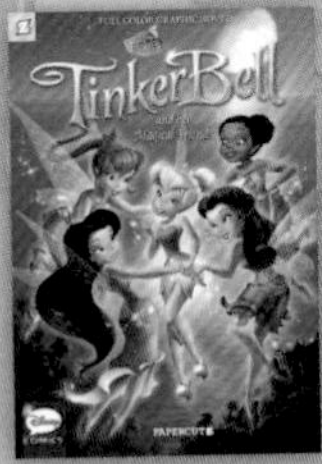

**Graphic Novel #18**
"Tinker Bell and her Magical Friends"

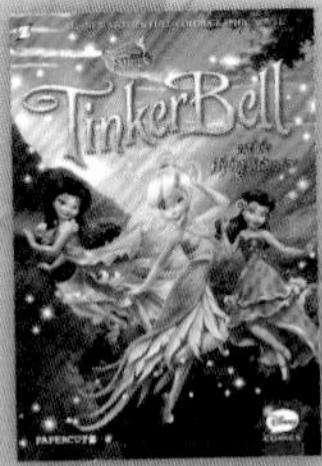

**Graphic Novel #19**
"Tinker Bell and the Flying Monster"

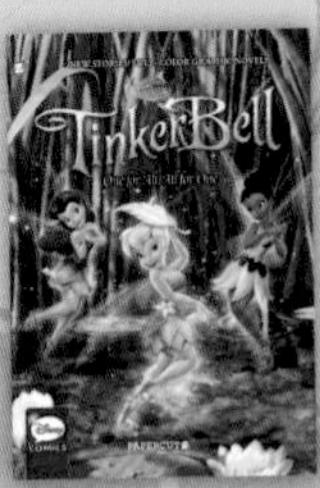

**Graphic Novel #20**
"Tinker Bell and a Far Too Secret Secret"

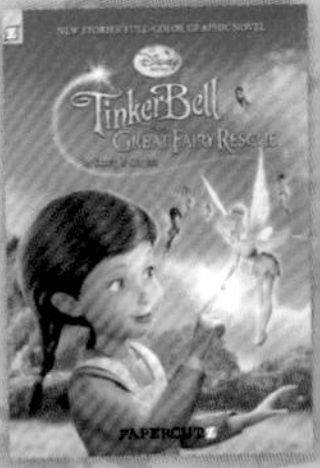

**Tinker Bell and the Great Fairy Rescue**

---

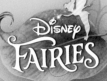

DISNEY FAIRIES graphic novels are available in paperback for $7.99 each; in hardcover for $12.99 each except #5, $6.99PB, $10.99HC, #6-14 are $7.99PB $11.99HC. Tinker Bell and the Great Fairy Rescue is $9.99 in hardcover only. Available at booksellers everywhere.

**See more at papercutz.com**

Or you can order from us: Please add $4.00 for postage and handling for first book, and add $1.00 for each additional book. Please make check payable to NBM Publishing. Send to: Papercutz, 160 Broadway, Suite 700, East Wing, New York, NY 10038 or call 800 886 1223 (9-6 EST M-F) MC-Visa-Amex accepted.

# DISNEY Fairies

# #20 "Tinker Bell and a Far-Too-Secret Secret"

## Contents

| | |
|---|---|
| A Secret to Share | 5 |
| A Silver Lining | 9 |
| Following A Dream | 13 |
| A Dazzling Delight | 17 |
| Water Games | 21 |
| A Far-Too-Secret Secret | 25 |
| A Question Of Taste | 29 |
| One For All, All For One | 33 |
| The Difficult Delivery | 37 |
| Mushroom Mayhem | 41 |
| Perfumed and Perfect | 45 |
| Good Night, Bunny! | 49 |
| Cooking Talent? | 53 |
| A Little Nap | 57 |
| Minnie & Daisy #2 Preview | 62 |

PAPERCUTZ™
NEW YORK

**Disney Fairies #20**
**"Tinker Bell and a Far-Too-Secret Secret"**

**"A Secret to Share"**
**Script:** Tea Orsi
**Layout and Cleanup:** Emilio Grasso
**Inks:** Santa Zangari
**Color:** Studio Kawaii

**"A Silver Lining"**
**Script:** Emanuela Portipiano
**Layout and Inks:** Sara Storino
**Cleanup:** Marino Gentile
**Color:** Studio Kawaii

**"Following A Dream"**
**Script:** Carlo Panaro
**Layout and Cleanup:** Monica Catalano
**Inks:** Roberta Zanotta
**Color:** Studio Kawaii

**"A Dazzling Delight"**
**Script:** Emanuela Portipiano
**Layout, Cleanup and Inks:** Monica Catalano
**Color:** Studio Kawaii

**"Water Games"**
**Script:** Emanuela Portipiano
**Layout, Cleanup and Inks:** Monica Catalano
**Color:** Studio Kawaii

**"A Far Too Secret Secret"**
**Script:** Emanuela Portipiano
**Layout:** Emilio Grasso
**Inks:** Santa Zangari
**Cleanup:** Emilio Grasso and Marino Gentile
**Color:** Studio Kawaii

**"A Question Of Taste"**
**Script:** Emanuela Portipiano
**Layout and Cleanup:** Manuela Razzi
**Inks:** Santa Zangari
**Color:** Studio Kawaii

**"One For All, All For One"**
**Script:** Tea Orsi
**Layout, Cleanup and Inks:** Sara Storino
**Color:** Studio Kawaii

**"The Difficult Delivery"**
**Script:** Tea Orsi
**Layout and Cleanup:** Sara Storino
**Inks:** Santa Zangari
**Color:** Studio Kawaii

**"Mushroom Mayhem"**
**Script:** Tea Orsi
**Layout and Cleanup:** Marino Gentile
**Inks:** Roberta Zanotta
**Color:** Studio Kawaii

**"Perfumed and Perfect"**
**Script:** Tea Orsi
**Layout:** Sara Storino
**Inks:** Santa Zangari
**Cleanup:** Marino Gentile
**Color:** Studio Kawaii

**"Good Night, Bunny!"**
**Script:** Tea Orsi
**Layout and Cleanup:** Marino Gentile
**Inks:** Santa Zangari
**Color:** Studio Kawaii

**"Cooking Talent?"**
**Script:** De Cunto Marta
**Layout and Cleanup:** Barone Gianluc
**Inks:** Santa Zangari
**Color:** Studio Kawaii

**"A Little Nap"**
**Script:** Silvia Lombardi
**Layout and Cleanup:** Sara Storino
**Inks:** Santa Zangari
**Color:** Studio Kawaii

**Minnie & Daisy #2 Preview**
**Script:** Silvia Gianatti
**Art:** Stefano De Lellis
**Inks:** Santa Zangari
**Color:** Angela Capolupo

**Production** – Dawn Guzzo
**Production Coordinator** – Sasha Kimiatek
**Editor** – Robert V. Conte
**Assistant Managing Editor** – Jeff Whitman
**Special Thanks to** – Carlotta Quattrocolo, Arianna Marchione, Krista Wong, and Eugene Paraszczuk at Disney Enterprises, Inc
Jim Salicrup
**Editor-in-Chief**

ISBN: 978-1-62991-784-9 Paperback Edition
ISBN: 978-1-62991-785-6 Hardcover Edition

Printed in Korea
Printed April 2017

Papercutz books may be purchased for business or promotional use.
For information on bulk purchases please contact Macmillan
Corporate and Premium Sales Department at (800) 221-7945 x5442.

Distributed by Macmillan
First Papercutz Printing

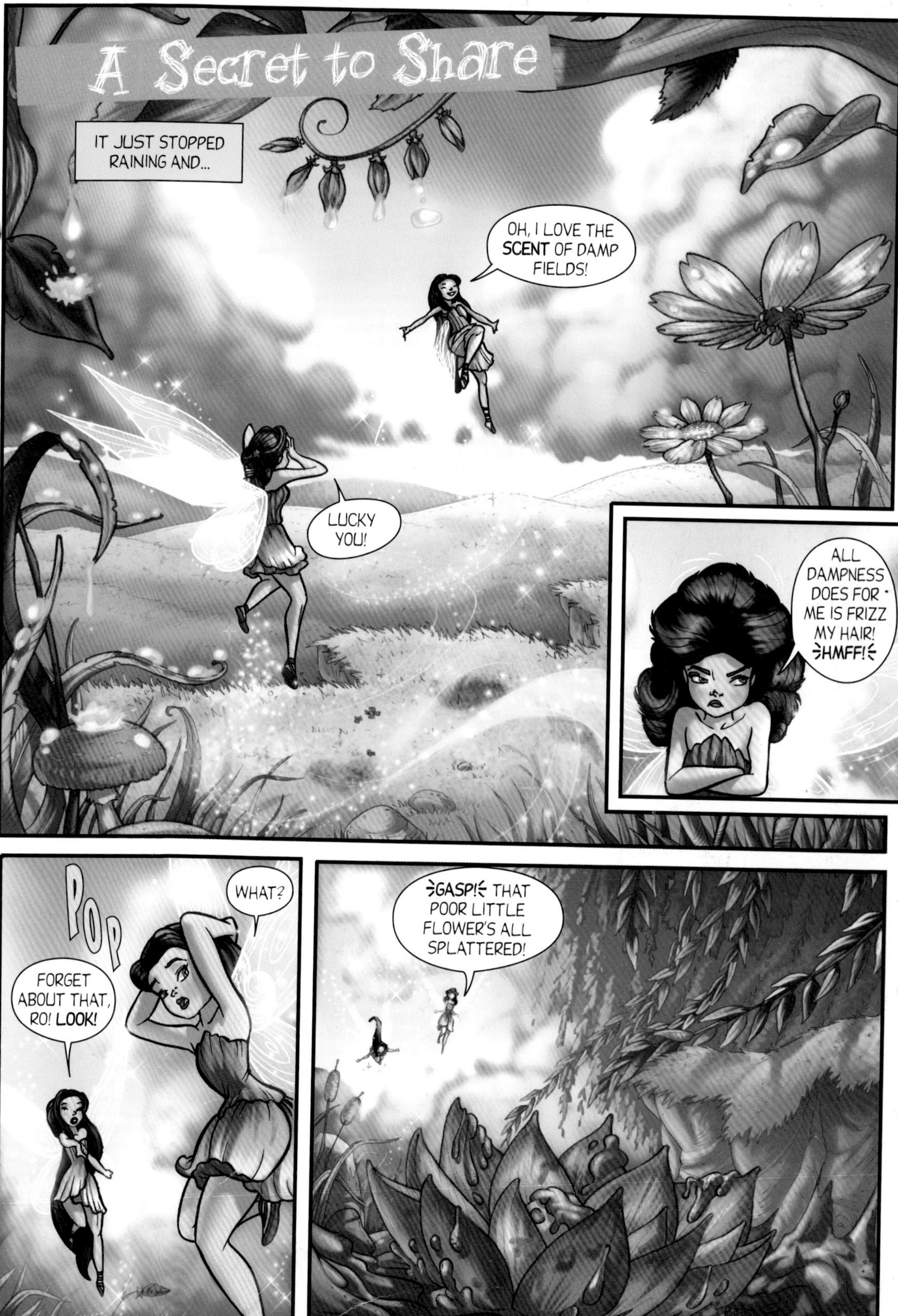
A Secret to Share
IT JUST STOPPED RAINING AND...
OH, I LOVE THE SCENT OF DAMP FIELDS!
LUCKY YOU!
ALL DAMPNESS DOES FOR ME IS FRIZZ MY HAIR! HMFF!
POP
WHAT?
FORGET ABOUT THAT, RO! LOOK!
GASP! THAT POOR LITTLE FLOWER'S ALL SPLATTERED!

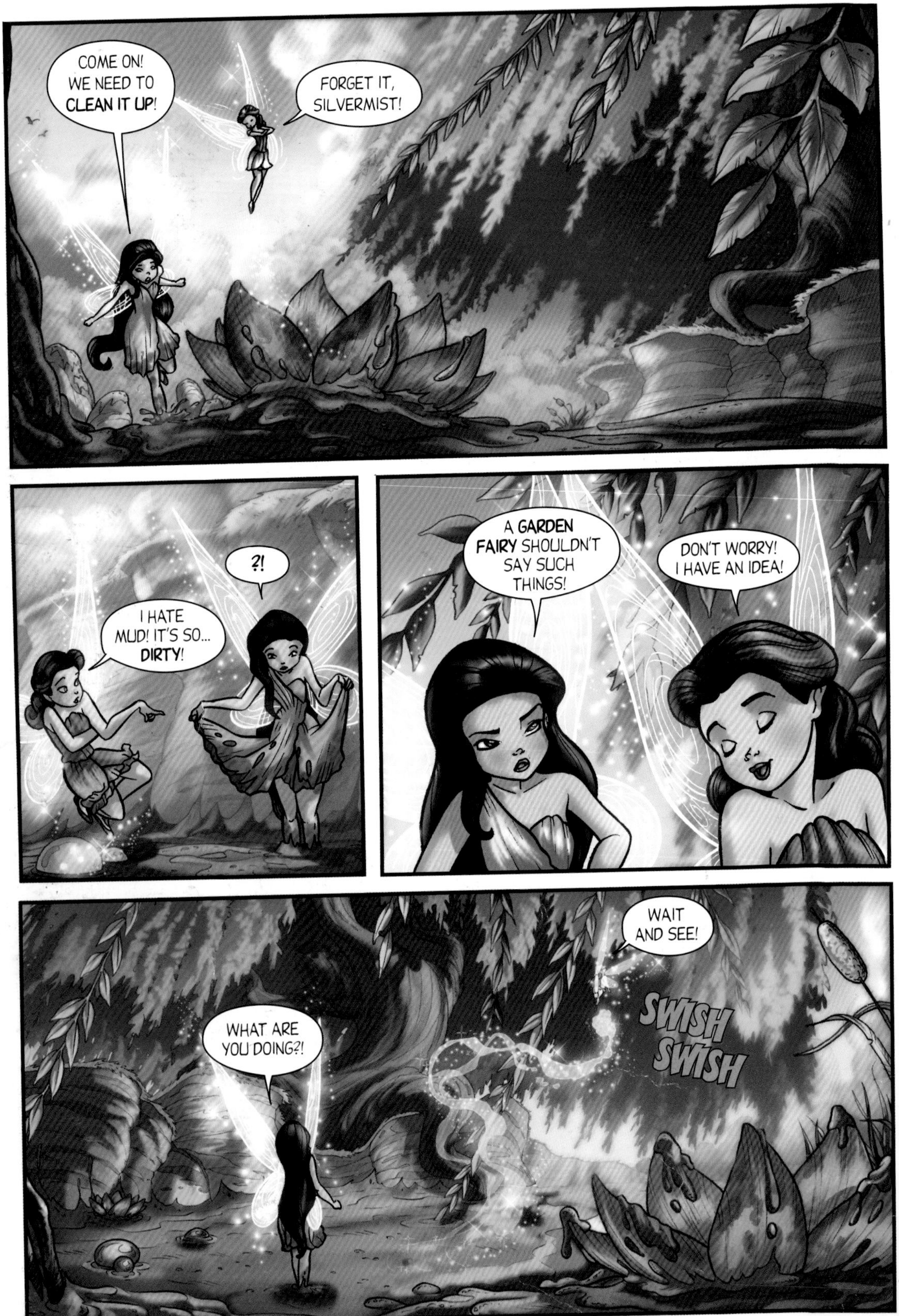
COME ON! WE NEED TO CLEAN IT UP!
FORGET IT, SILVERMIST!
I HATE MUD! IT'S SO... DIRTY!
?!
A GARDEN FAIRY SHOULDN'T SAY SUCH THINGS!
DON'T WORRY! I HAVE AN IDEA!
WAIT AND SEE!
WHAT ARE YOU DOING?!
SWISH SWISH

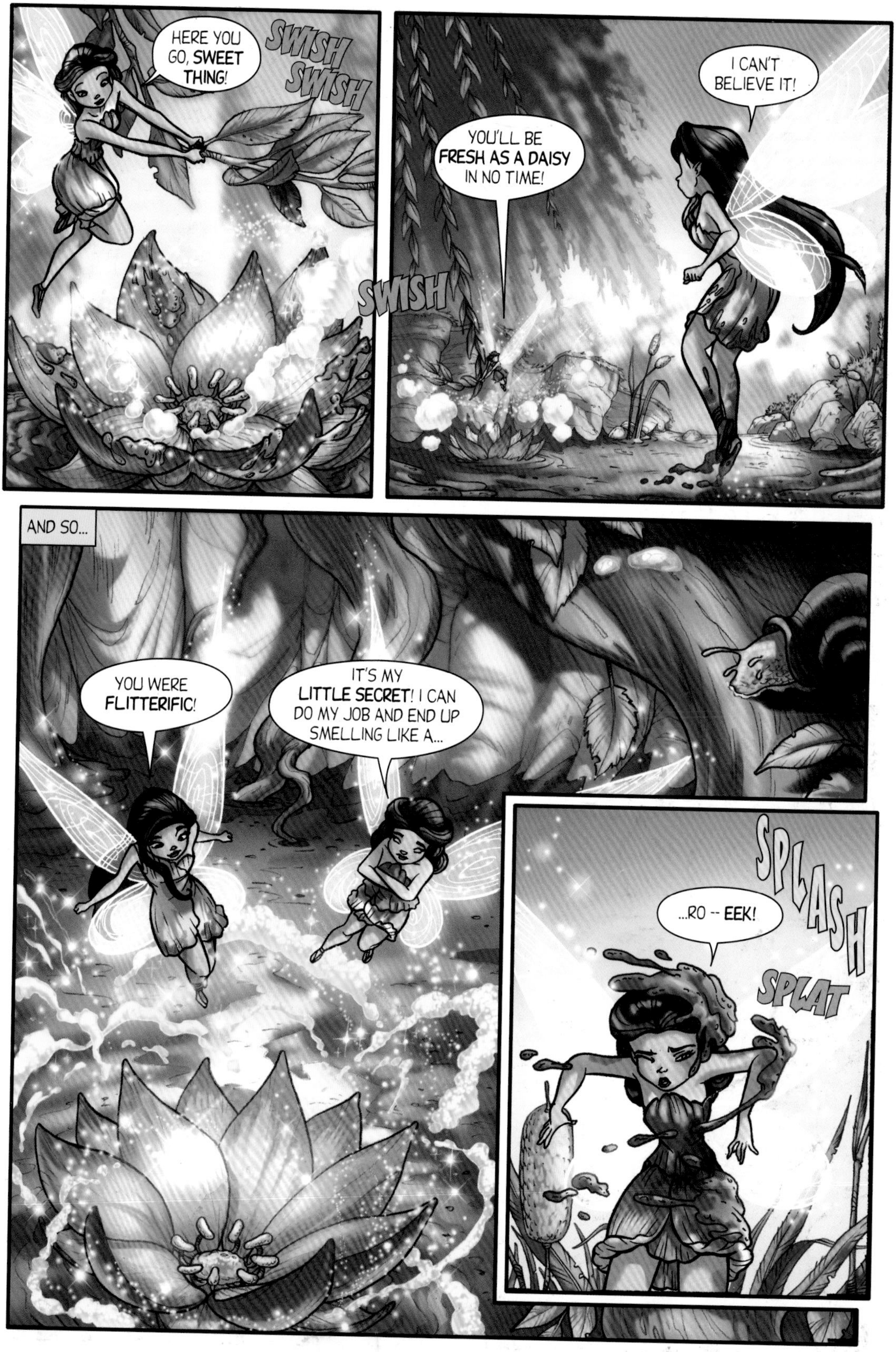
HERE YOU GO, SWEET THING!
SWISH SWISH
I CAN'T BELIEVE IT!
YOU'LL BE FRESH AS A DAISY IN NO TIME!
SWISH
AND SO...
YOU WERE FLITTERIFIC!
IT'S MY LITTLE SECRET! I CAN DO MY JOB AND END UP SMELLING LIKE A...
SPLASH
...RO -- EEK!
SPLAT

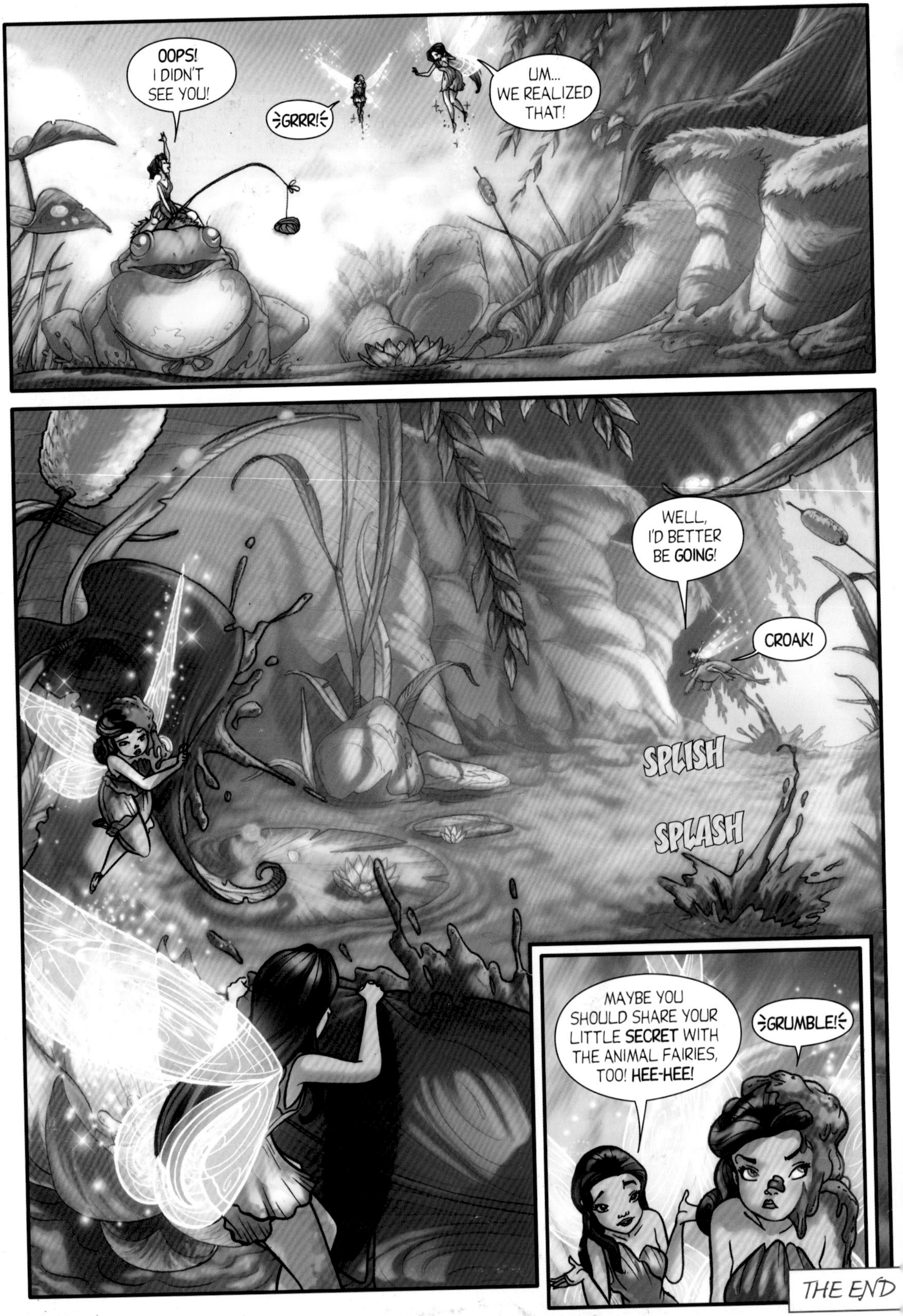
OOPS! I DIDN'T SEE YOU!
GRRR!
UM... WE REALIZED THAT!
WELL, I'D BETTER BE GOING!
CROAK!
SPLISH
SPLASH
MAYBE YOU SHOULD SHARE YOUR LITTLE SECRET WITH THE ANIMAL FAIRIES, TOO! HEE-HEE!
GRUMBLE!
THE END

# A Silver Lining

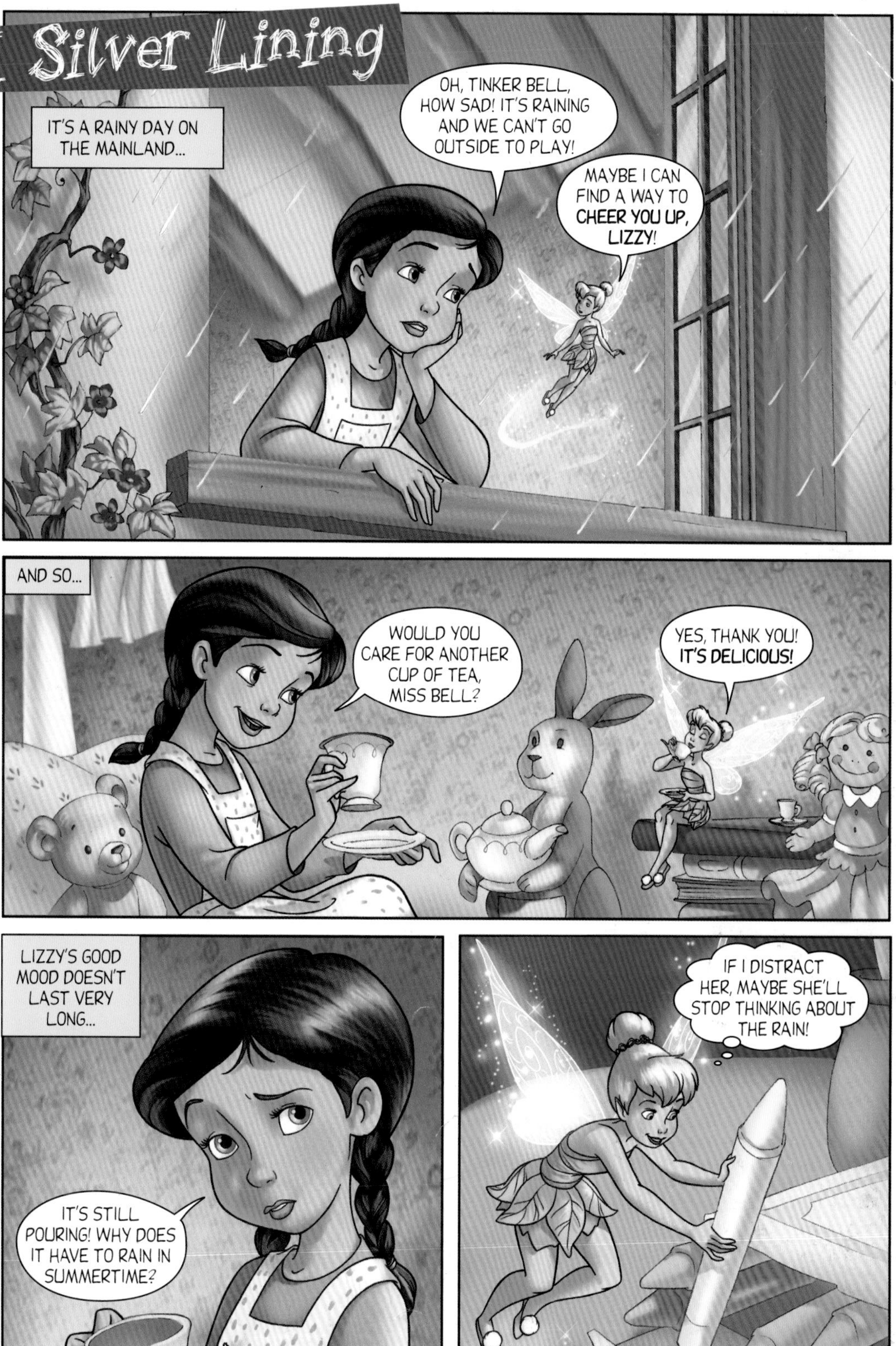
IT'S A RAINY DAY ON THE MAINLAND...
OH, TINKER BELL, HOW SAD! IT'S RAINING AND WE CAN'T GO OUTSIDE TO PLAY!
MAYBE I CAN FIND A WAY TO **CHEER YOU UP, LIZZY**!
AND SO...
WOULD YOU CARE FOR ANOTHER CUP OF TEA, MISS BELL?
YES, THANK YOU! **IT'S DELICIOUS!**
LIZZY'S GOOD MOOD DOESN'T LAST VERY LONG...
IT'S STILL POURING! WHY DOES IT HAVE TO RAIN IN SUMMERTIME?
IF I DISTRACT HER, MAYBE SHE'LL STOP THINKING ABOUT THE RAIN!

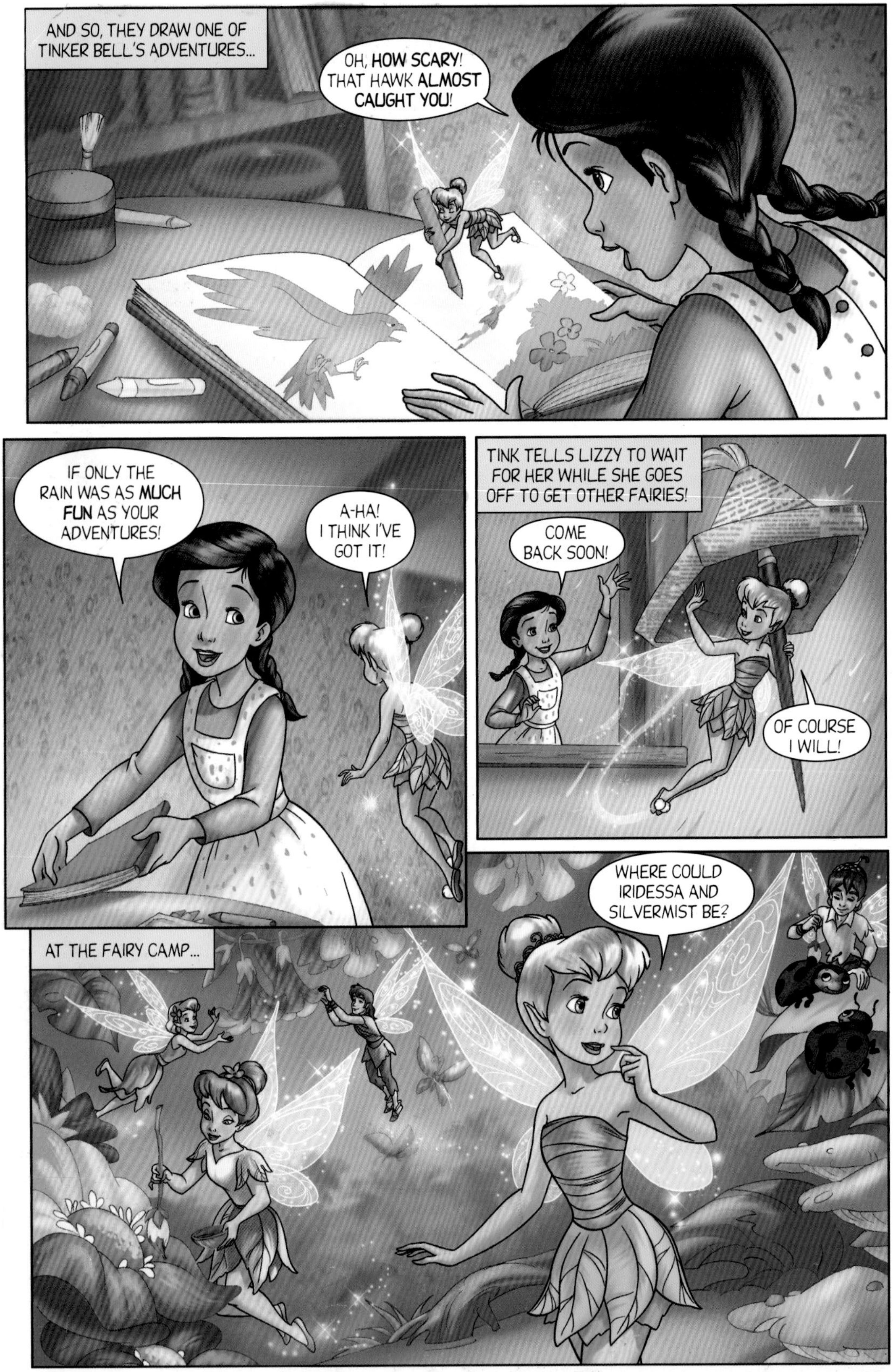
AND SO, THEY DRAW ONE OF TINKER BELL'S ADVENTURES...
OH, HOW SCARY! THAT HAWK ALMOST CAUGHT YOU!
IF ONLY THE RAIN WAS AS MUCH FUN AS YOUR ADVENTURES!
A-HA! I THINK I'VE GOT IT!
TINK TELLS LIZZY TO WAIT FOR HER WHILE SHE GOES OFF TO GET OTHER FAIRIES!
COME BACK SOON!
OF COURSE I WILL!
AT THE FAIRY CAMP...
WHERE COULD IRIDESSA AND SILVERMIST BE?

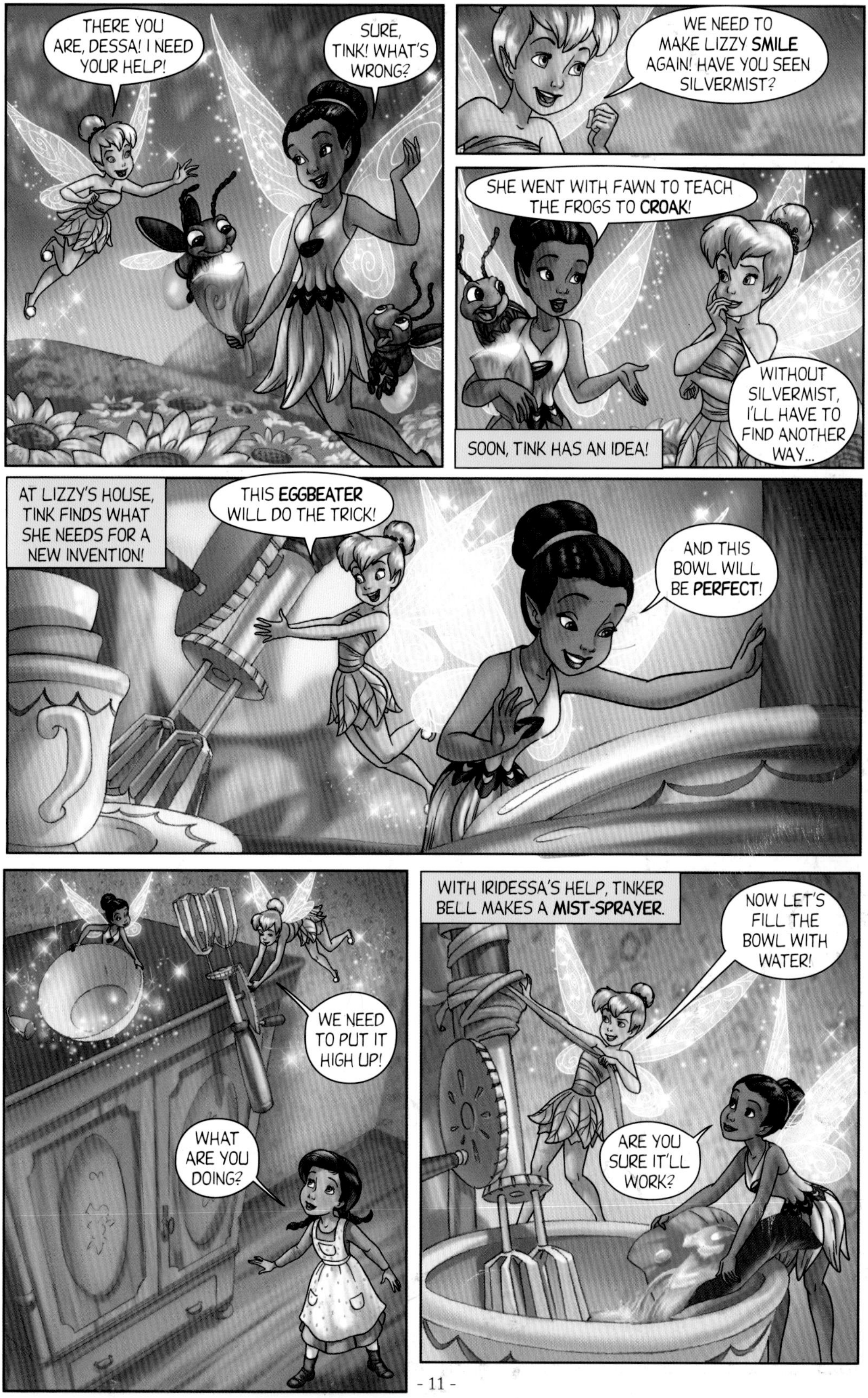
THERE YOU ARE, DESSA! I NEED YOUR HELP!
SURE, TINK! WHAT'S WRONG?
WE NEED TO MAKE LIZZY **SMILE** AGAIN! HAVE YOU SEEN SILVERMIST?
SHE WENT WITH FAWN TO TEACH THE FROGS TO **CROAK**!
WITHOUT SILVERMIST, I'LL HAVE TO FIND ANOTHER WAY...
SOON, TINK HAS AN IDEA!
AT LIZZY'S HOUSE, TINK FINDS WHAT SHE NEEDS FOR A NEW INVENTION!
THIS **EGGBEATER** WILL DO THE TRICK!
AND THIS BOWL WILL BE **PERFECT**!
WE NEED TO PUT IT HIGH UP!
WHAT ARE YOU DOING?
WITH IRIDESSA'S HELP, TINKER BELL MAKES A **MIST-SPRAYER**.
NOW LET'S FILL THE BOWL WITH WATER!
ARE YOU SURE IT'LL WORK?

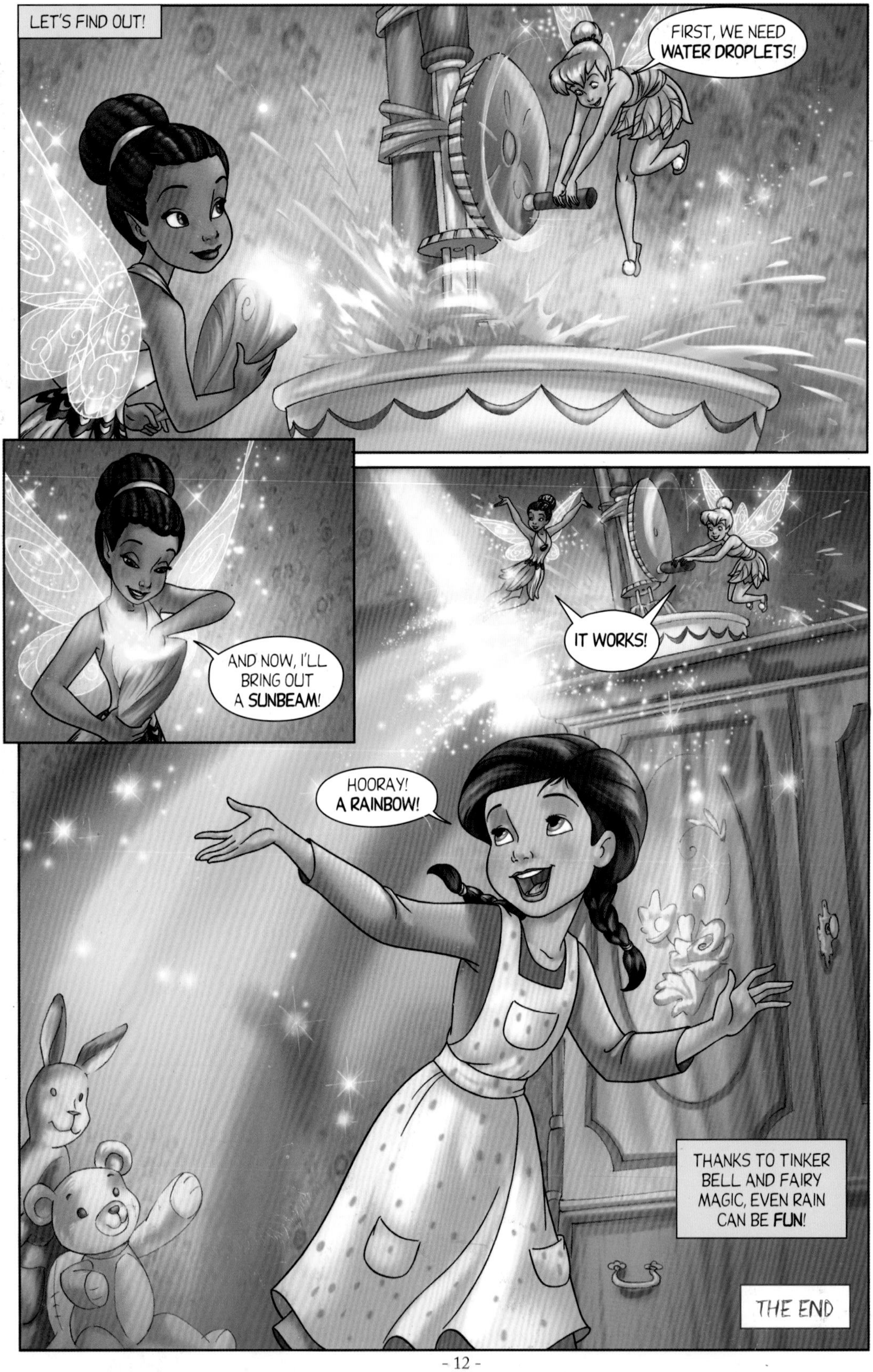

LET'S FIND OUT!
FIRST, WE NEED **WATER DROPLETS**!
AND NOW, I'LL BRING OUT A **SUNBEAM**!
IT WORKS!
HOORAY! **A RAINBOW**!
THANKS TO TINKER BELL AND FAIRY MAGIC, EVEN RAIN CAN BE **FUN**!
THE END

# Following a Dream

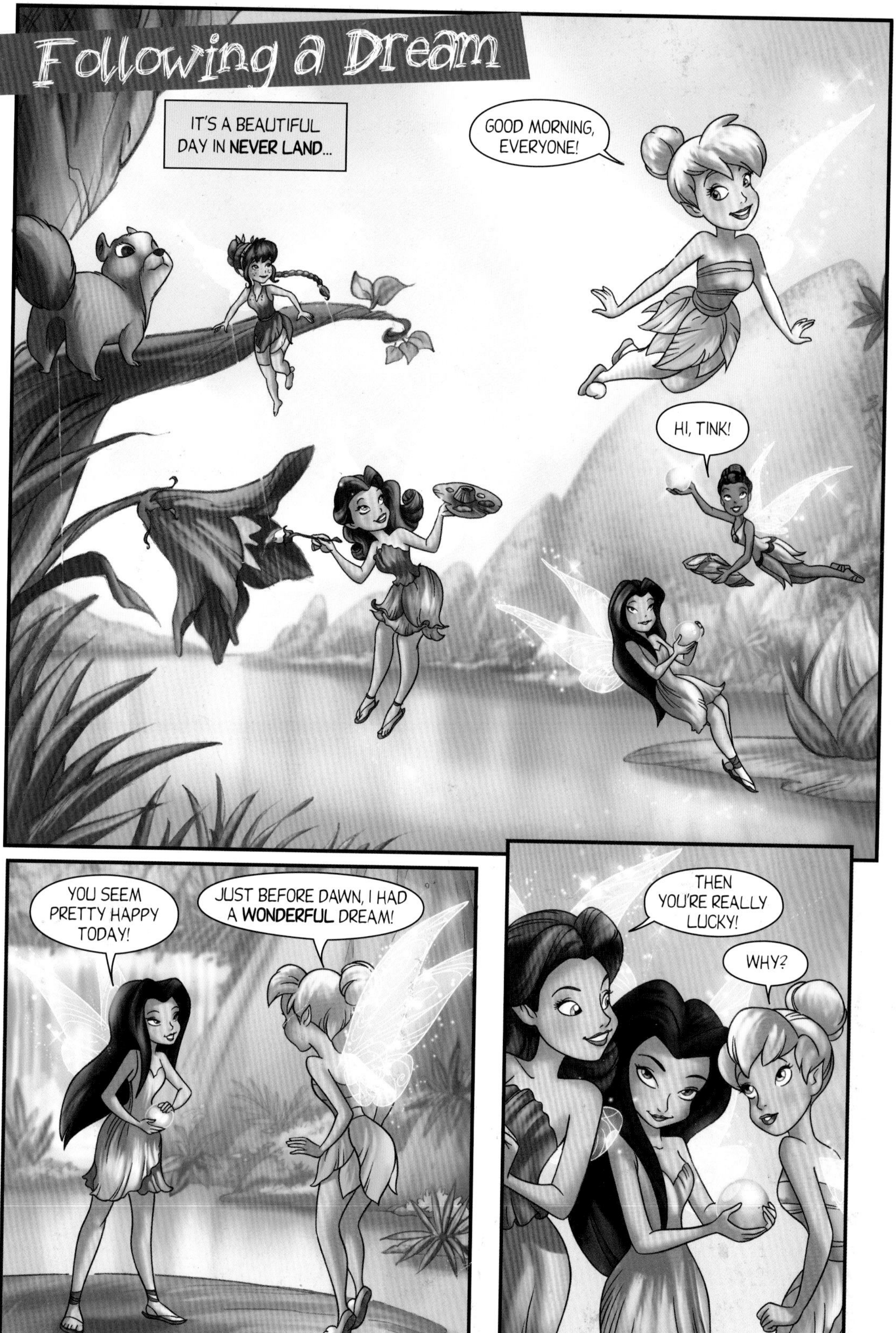

IT'S A BEAUTIFUL DAY IN NEVER LAND...
GOOD MORNING, EVERYONE!
HI, TINK!
YOU SEEM PRETTY HAPPY TODAY!
JUST BEFORE DAWN, I HAD A WONDERFUL DREAM!
THEN YOU'RE REALLY LUCKY!
WHY?

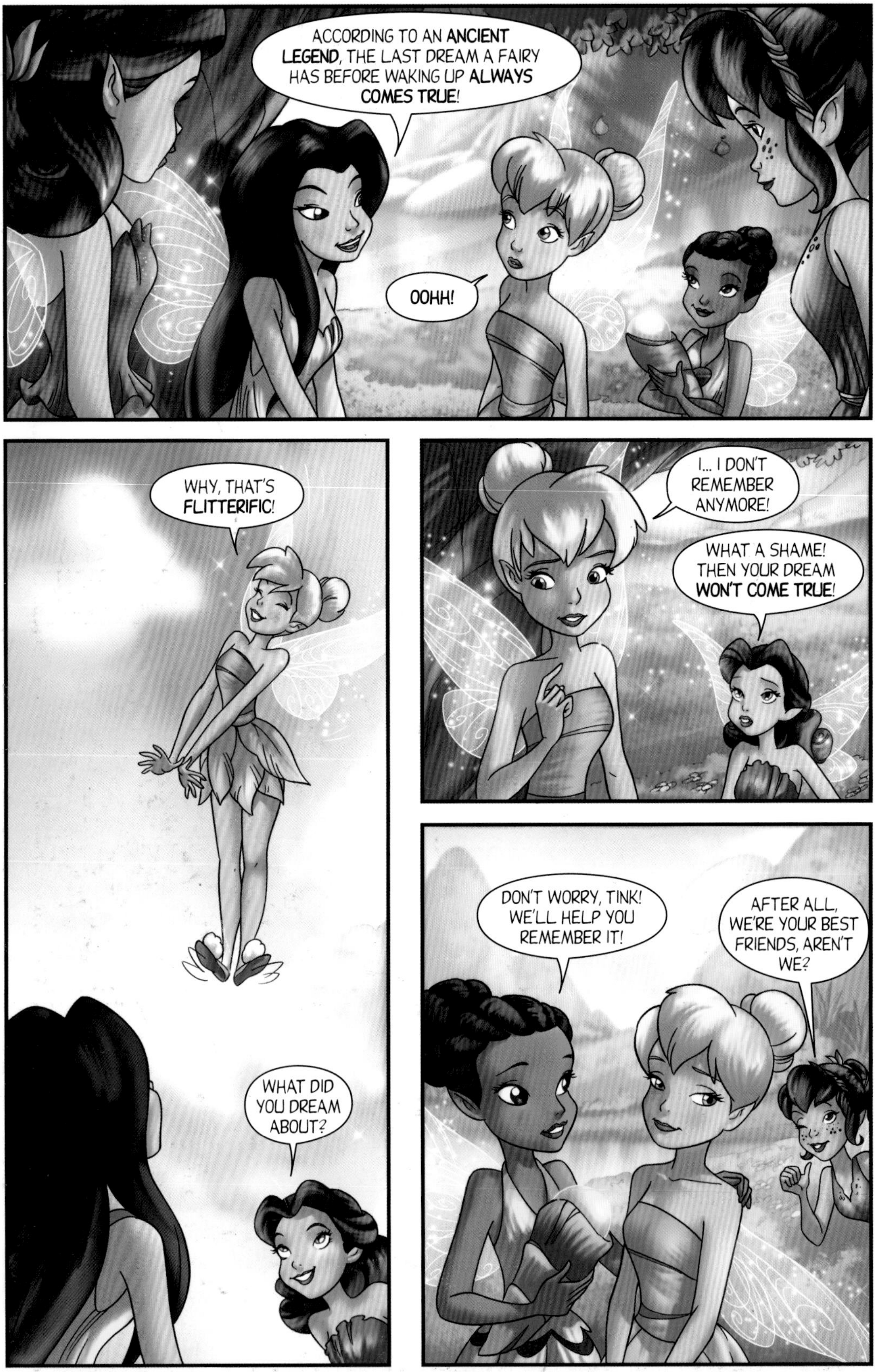
ACCORDING TO AN ANCIENT LEGEND, THE LAST DREAM A FAIRY HAS BEFORE WAKING UP ALWAYS COMES TRUE!
OOHH!
WHY, THAT'S FLITTERIFIC!
WHAT DID YOU DREAM ABOUT?
I... I DON'T REMEMBER ANYMORE!
WHAT A SHAME! THEN YOUR DREAM WON'T COME TRUE!
DON'T WORRY, TINK! WE'LL HELP YOU REMEMBER IT!
AFTER ALL, WE'RE YOUR BEST FRIENDS, AREN'T WE?

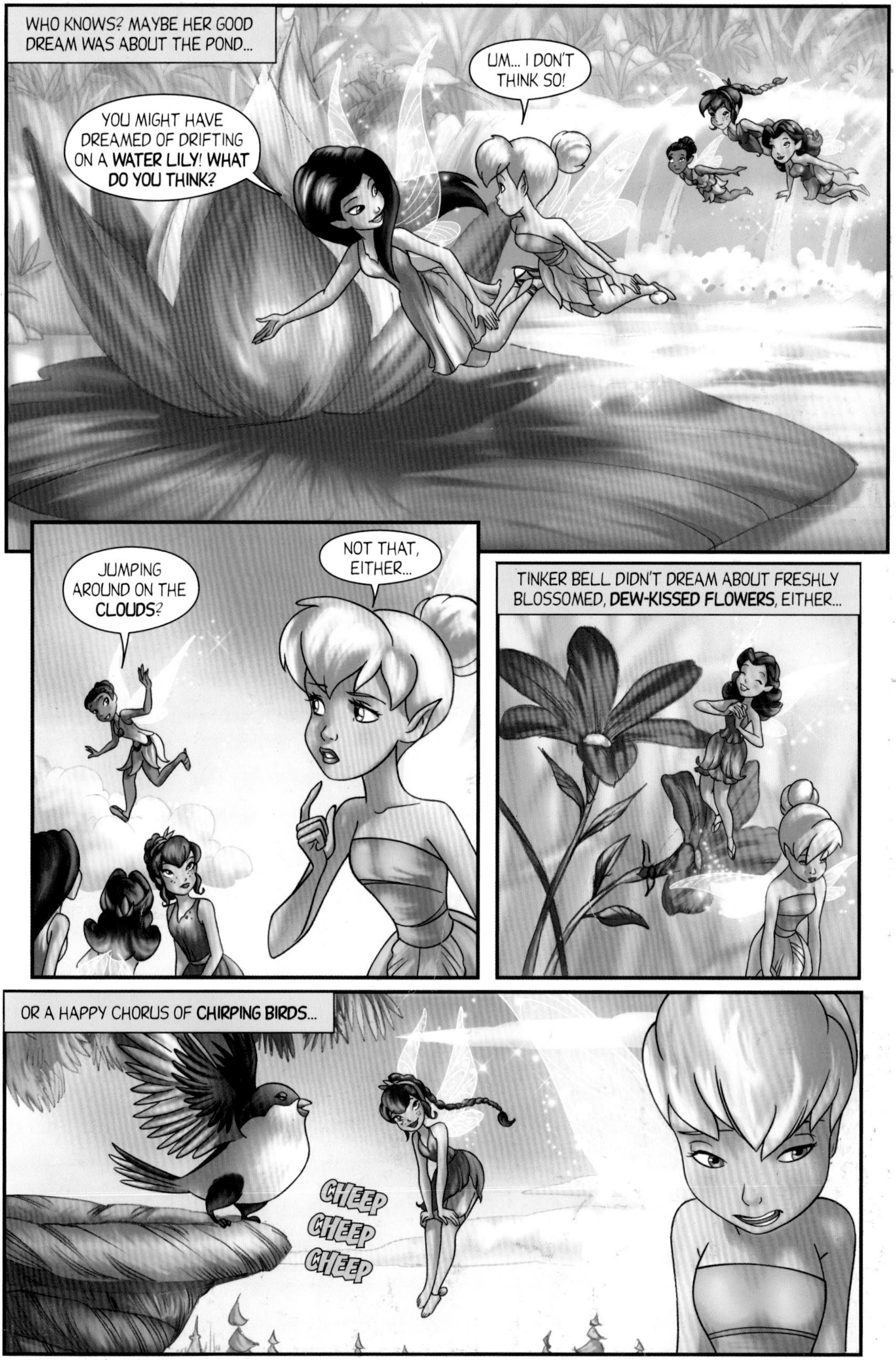

WHO KNOWS? MAYBE HER GOOD DREAM WAS ABOUT THE POND...
YOU MIGHT HAVE DREAMED OF DRIFTING ON A WATER LILY! WHAT DO YOU THINK?
UM... I DON'T THINK SO!
JUMPING AROUND ON THE CLOUDS?
NOT THAT, EITHER...
TINKER BELL DIDN'T DREAM ABOUT FRESHLY BLOSSOMED, DEW-KISSED FLOWERS, EITHER...
OR A HAPPY CHORUS OF CHIRPING BIRDS...
CHEEP
CHEEP
CHEEP

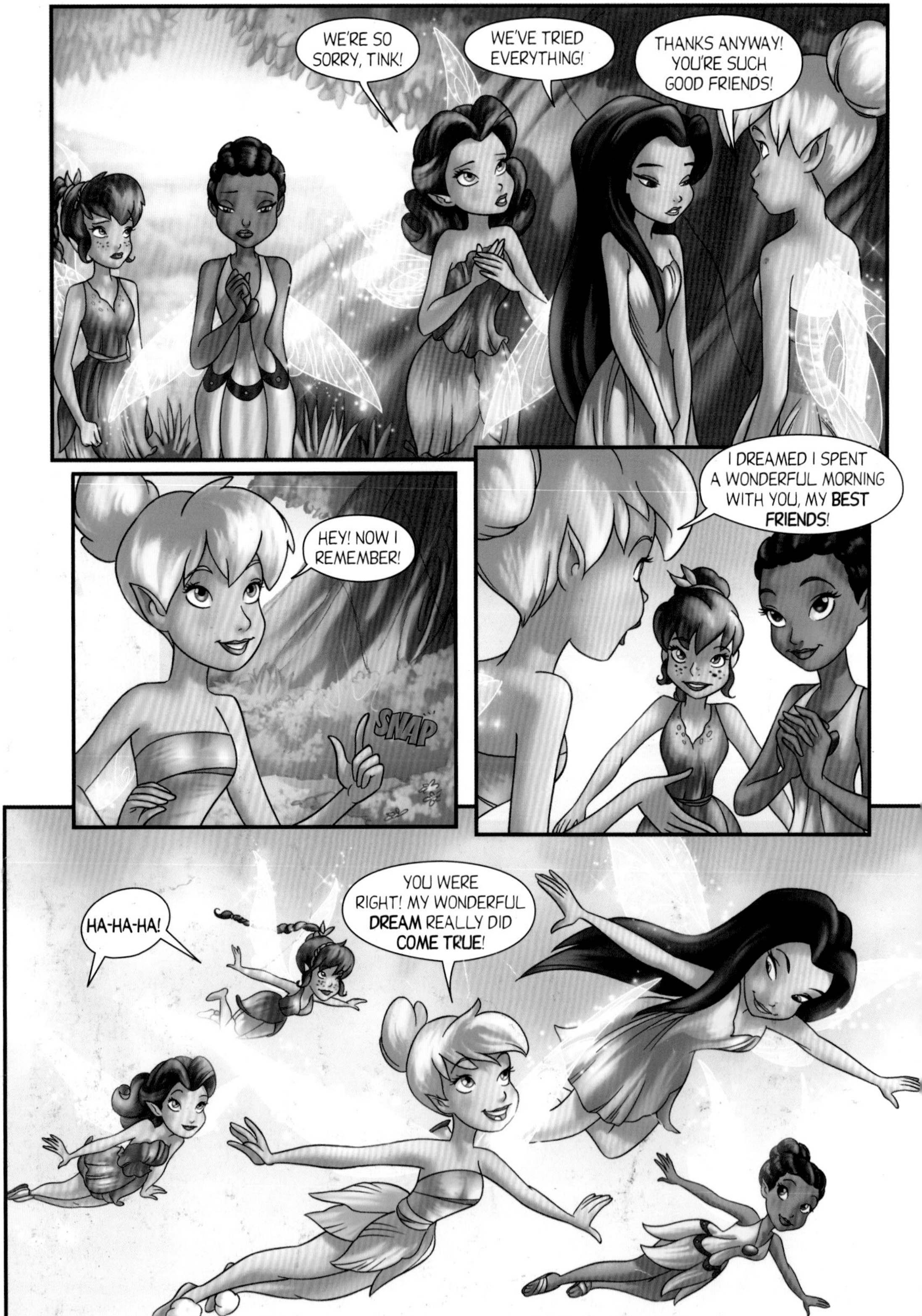
WE'RE SO SORRY, TINK!
WE'VE TRIED EVERYTHING!
THANKS ANYWAY! YOU'RE SUCH GOOD FRIENDS!
HEY! NOW I REMEMBER!
SNAP
I DREAMED I SPENT A WONDERFUL MORNING WITH YOU, MY BEST FRIENDS!
HA-HA-HA!
YOU WERE RIGHT! MY WONDERFUL DREAM REALLY DID COME TRUE!
THE END

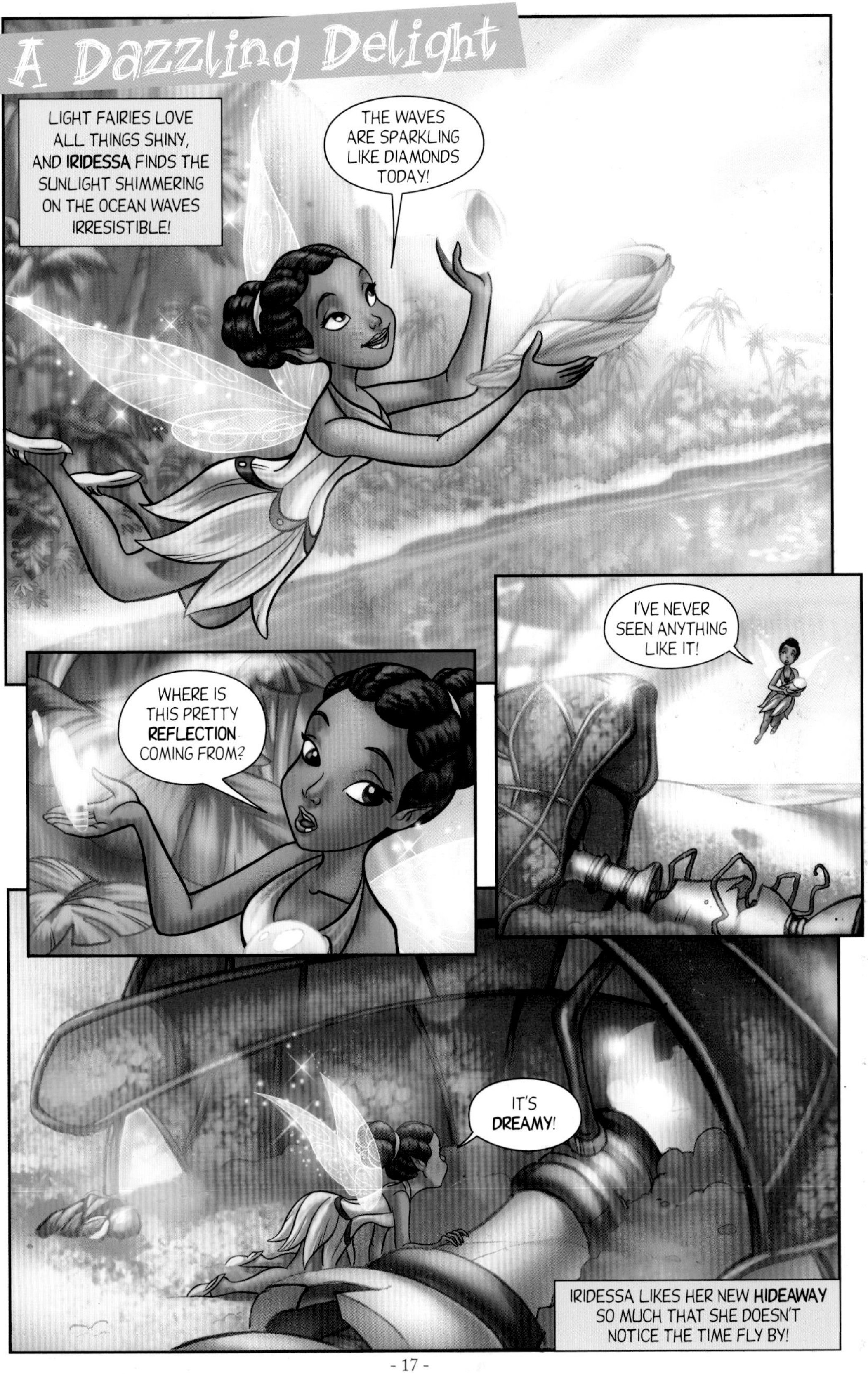
A Dazzling Delight
LIGHT FAIRIES LOVE ALL THINGS SHINY, AND IRIDESSA FINDS THE SUNLIGHT SHIMMERING ON THE OCEAN WAVES IRRESISTIBLE!
THE WAVES ARE SPARKLING LIKE DIAMONDS TODAY!
WHERE IS THIS PRETTY REFLECTION COMING FROM?
I'VE NEVER SEEN ANYTHING LIKE IT!
IT'S DREAMY!
IRIDESSA LIKES HER NEW HIDEAWAY SO MUCH THAT SHE DOESN'T NOTICE THE TIME FLY BY!

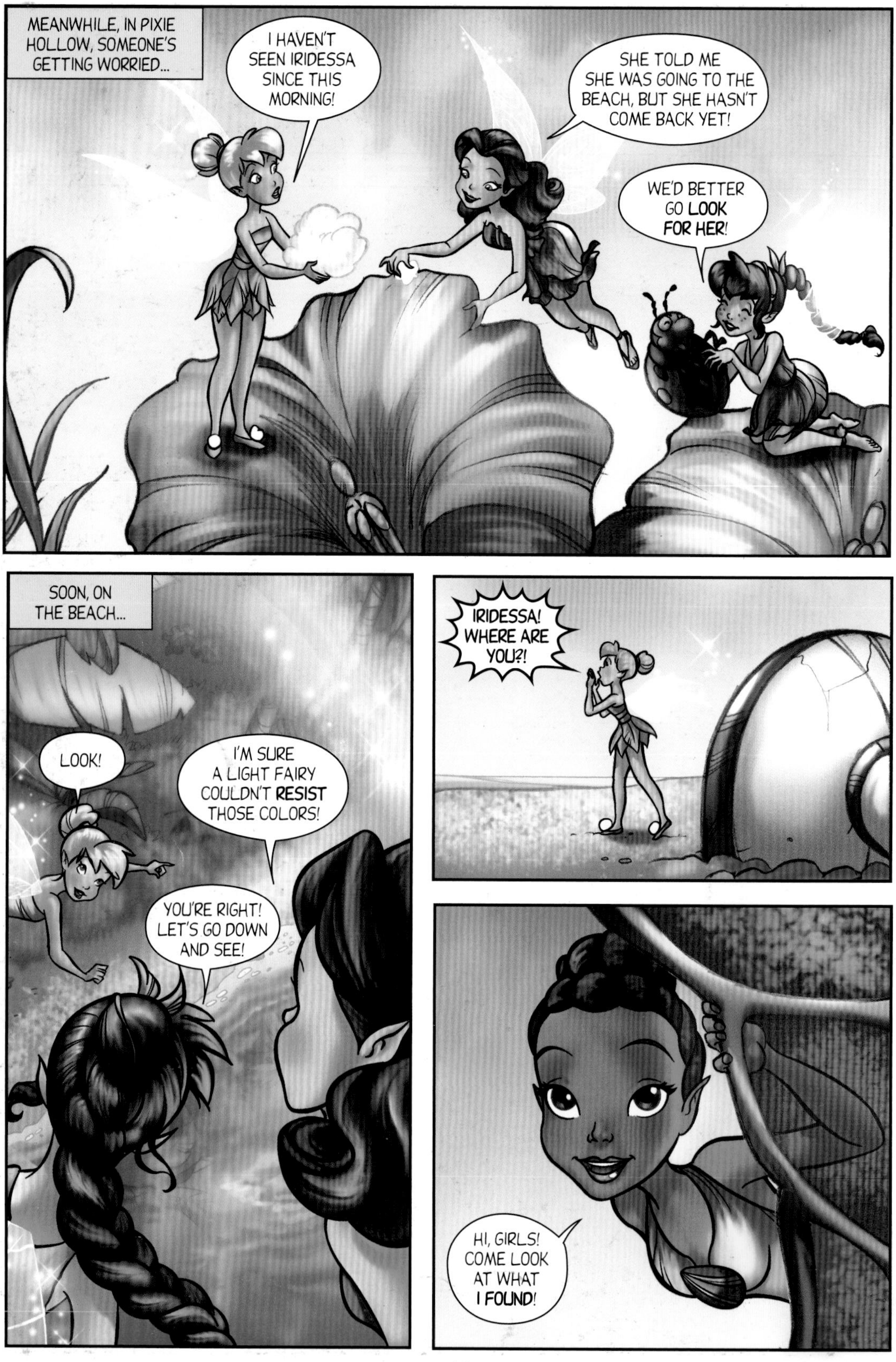
MEANWHILE, IN PIXIE HOLLOW, SOMEONE'S GETTING WORRIED...
I HAVEN'T SEEN IRIDESSA SINCE THIS MORNING!
SHE TOLD ME SHE WAS GOING TO THE BEACH, BUT SHE HASN'T COME BACK YET!
WE'D BETTER GO LOOK FOR HER!
SOON, ON THE BEACH...
LOOK!
I'M SURE A LIGHT FAIRY COULDN'T RESIST THOSE COLORS!
YOU'RE RIGHT! LET'S GO DOWN AND SEE!
IRIDESSA! WHERE ARE YOU?!
HI, GIRLS! COME LOOK AT WHAT I FOUND!

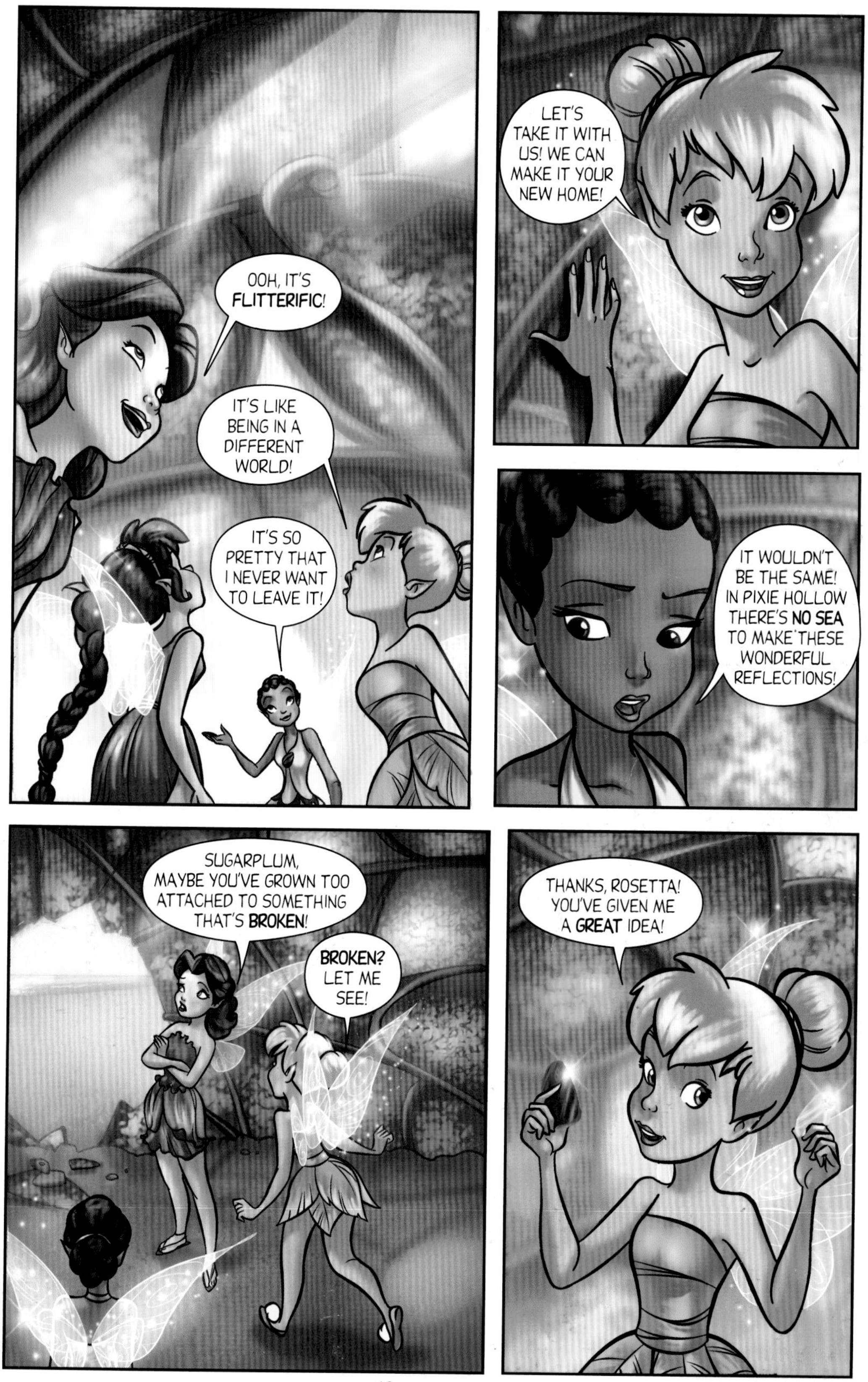
OOH, IT'S FLITTERIFIC!
IT'S LIKE BEING IN A DIFFERENT WORLD!
IT'S SO PRETTY THAT I NEVER WANT TO LEAVE IT!
LET'S TAKE IT WITH US! WE CAN MAKE IT YOUR NEW HOME!
IT WOULDN'T BE THE SAME! IN PIXIE HOLLOW THERE'S NO SEA TO MAKE THESE WONDERFUL REFLECTIONS!
SUGARPLUM, MAYBE YOU'VE GROWN TOO ATTACHED TO SOMETHING THAT'S BROKEN!
BROKEN? LET ME SEE!
THANKS, ROSETTA! YOU'VE GIVEN ME A GREAT IDEA!

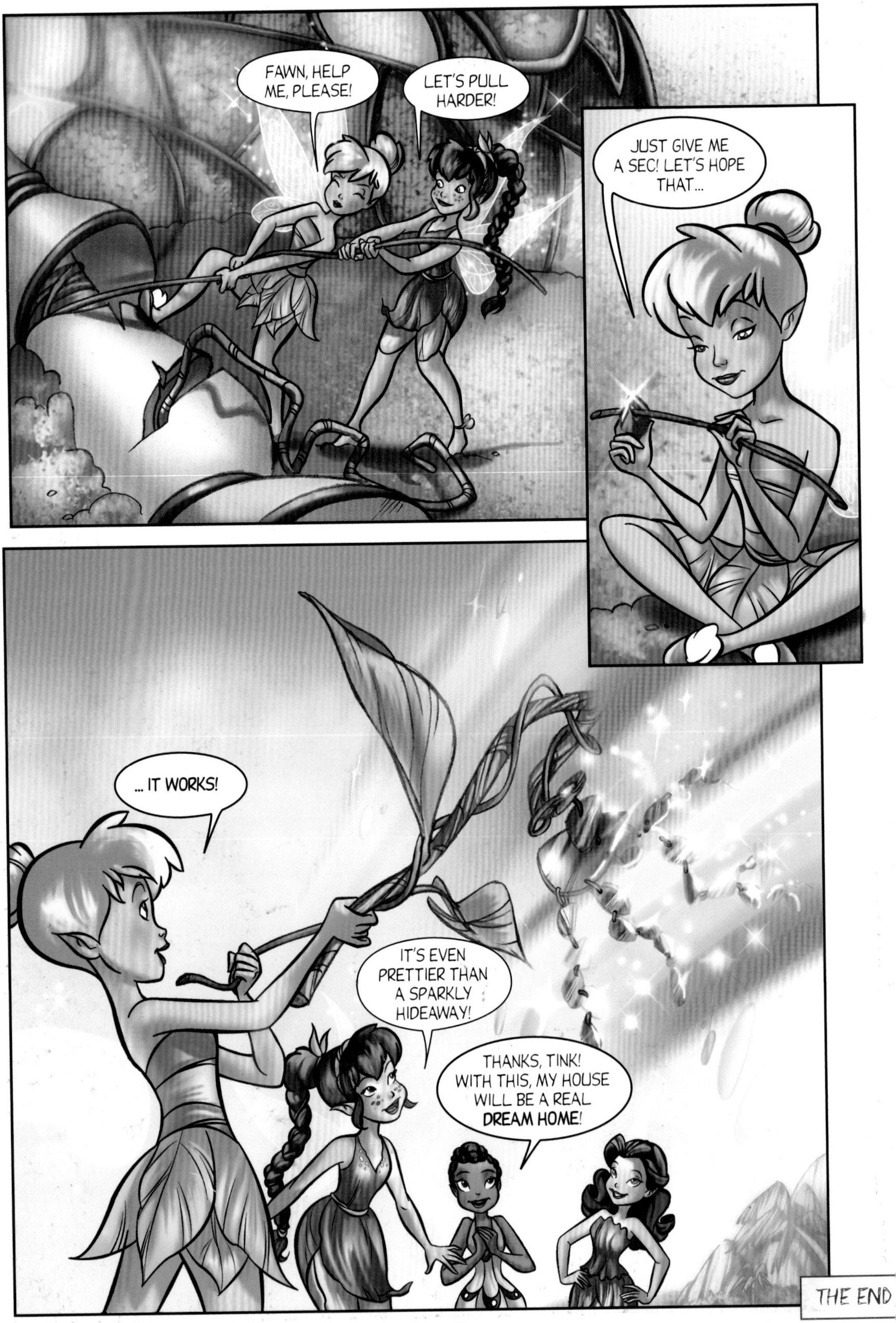
FAWN, HELP ME, PLEASE!
LET'S PULL HARDER!
JUST GIVE ME A SEC! LET'S HOPE THAT...
... IT WORKS!
IT'S EVEN PRETTIER THAN A SPARKLY HIDEAWAY!
THANKS, TINK! WITH THIS, MY HOUSE WILL BE A REAL **DREAM HOME**!
THE END

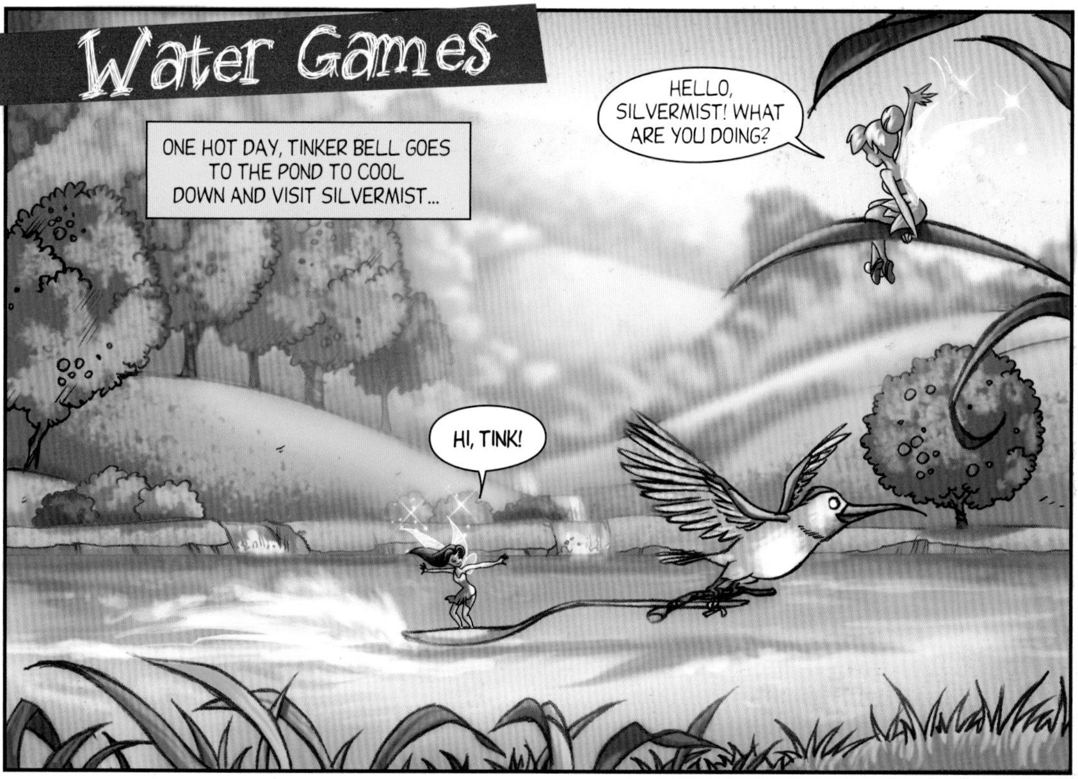
Water Games
ONE HOT DAY, TINKER BELL GOES TO THE POND TO COOL DOWN AND VISIT SILVERMIST...
HELLO, SILVERMIST! WHAT ARE YOU DOING?
HI, TINK!

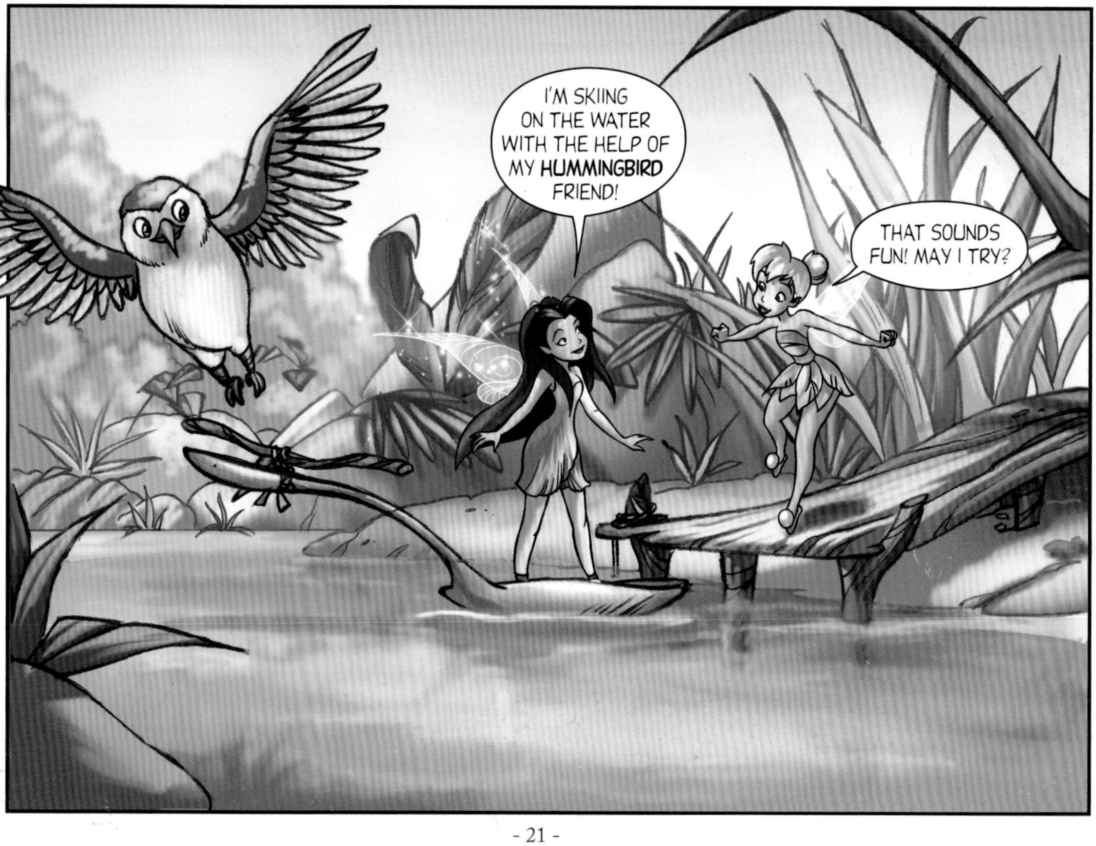
I'M SKIING ON THE WATER WITH THE HELP OF MY **HUMMINGBIRD** FRIEND!
THAT SOUNDS FUN! MAY I TRY?

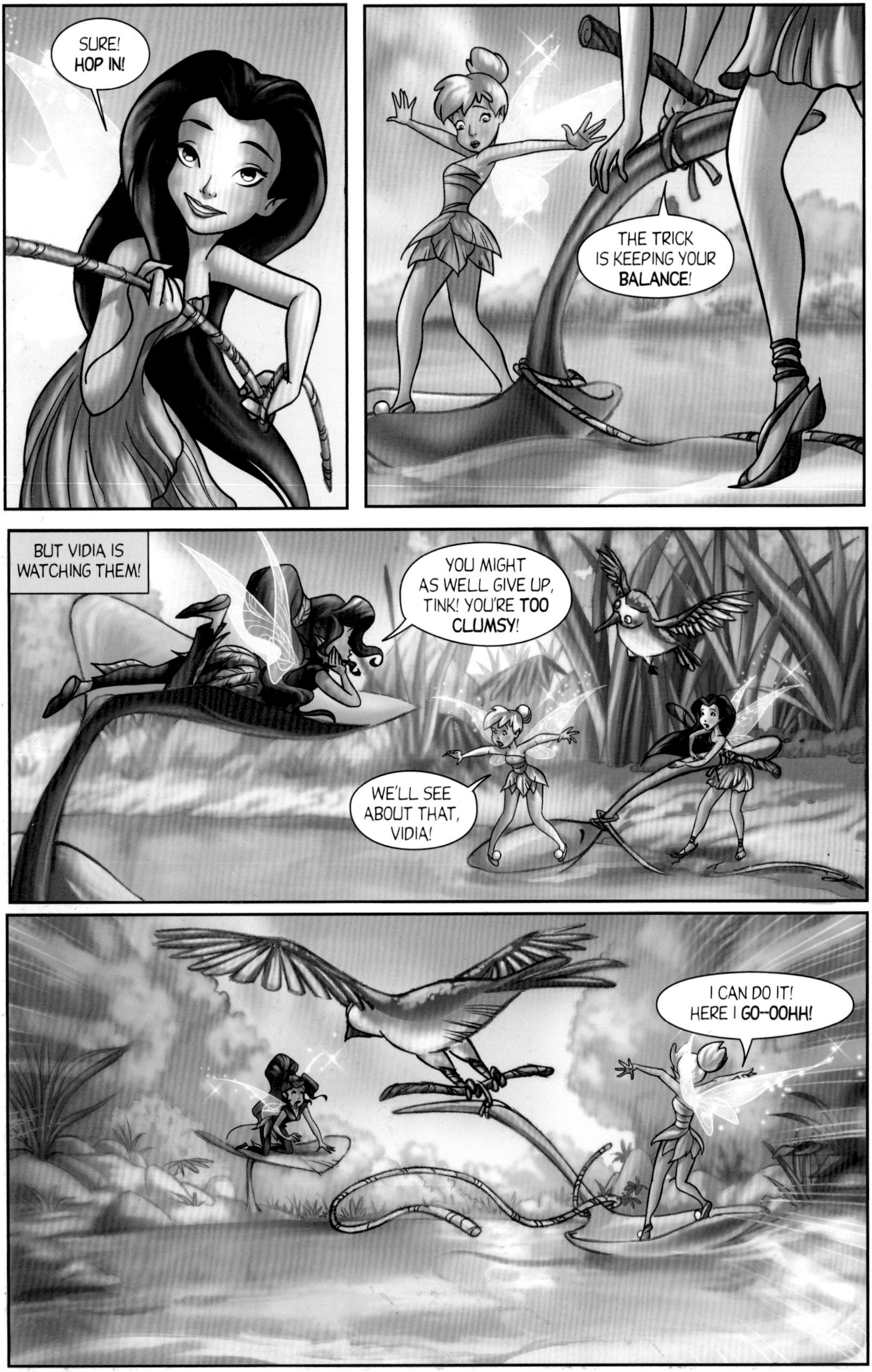
SURE! HOP IN!
THE TRICK IS KEEPING YOUR BALANCE!
BUT VIDIA IS WATCHING THEM!
YOU MIGHT AS WELL GIVE UP, TINK! YOU'RE TOO CLUMSY!
WE'LL SEE ABOUT THAT, VIDIA!
I CAN DO IT! HERE I GO--OOHH!

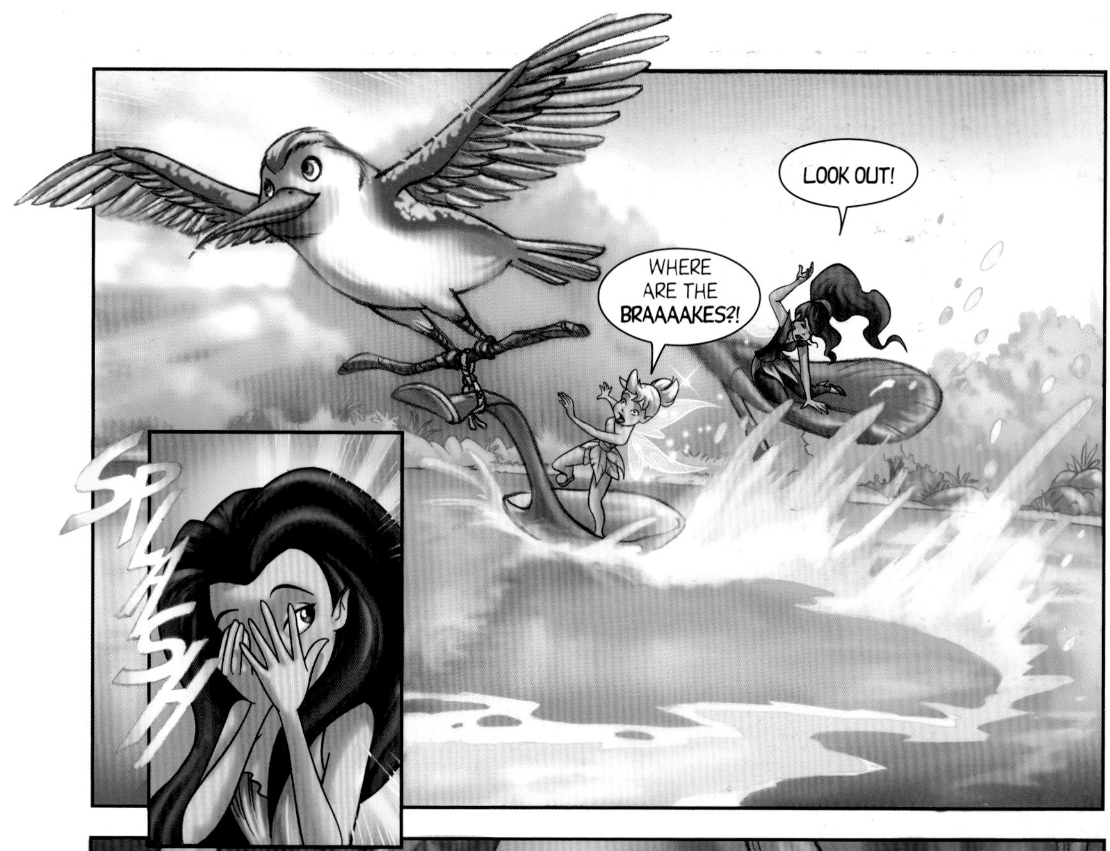
LOOK OUT!
WHERE ARE THE BRAAAAKES?!
SPLASH

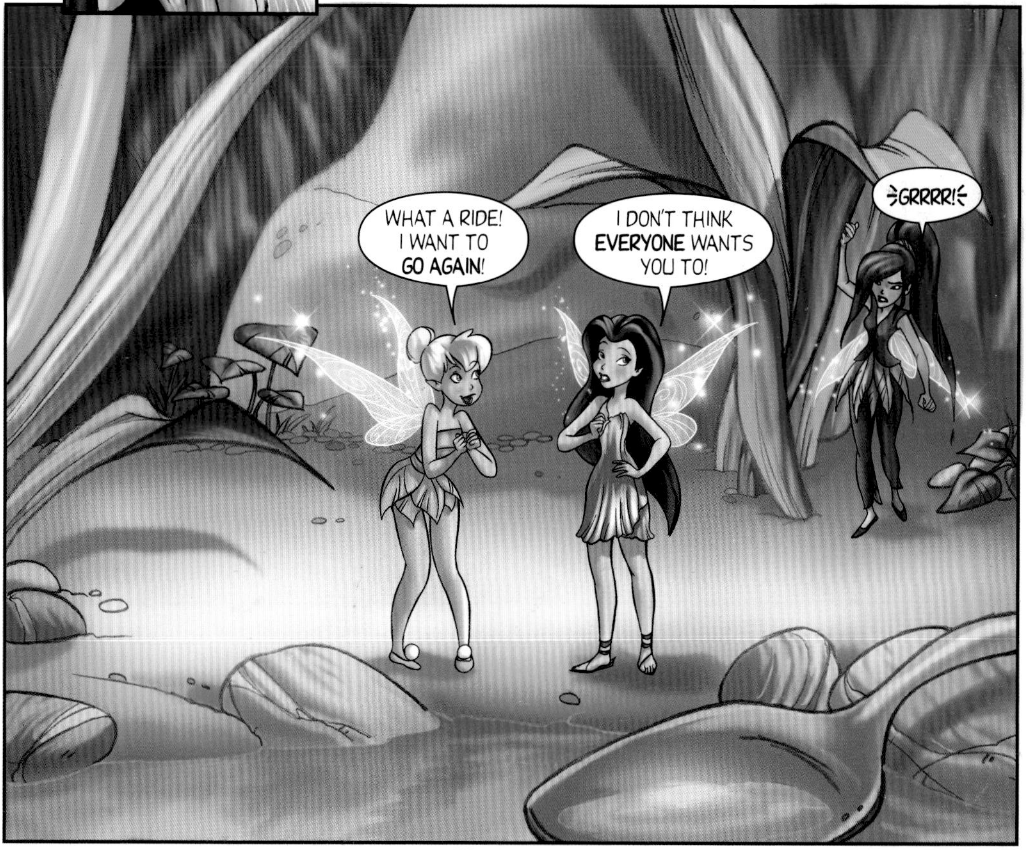
WHAT A RIDE! I WANT TO GO AGAIN!
I DON'T THINK EVERYONE WANTS YOU TO!
GRRRR!

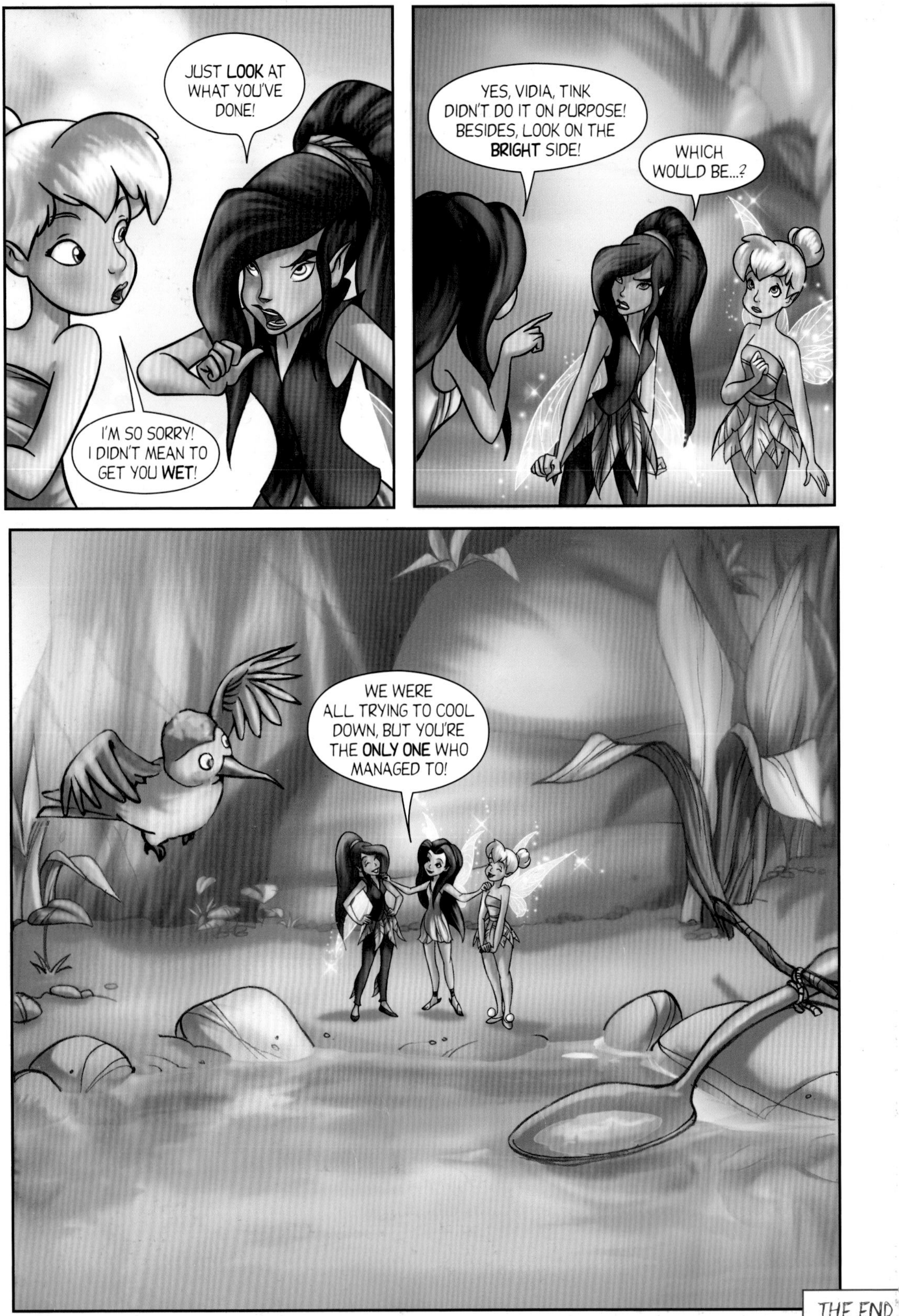
JUST **LOOK** AT WHAT YOU'VE DONE!
I'M SO SORRY! I DIDN'T MEAN TO GET YOU **WET**!
YES, VIDIA, TINK DIDN'T DO IT ON PURPOSE! BESIDES, LOOK ON THE **BRIGHT** SIDE!
WHICH WOULD BE...?
WE WERE ALL TRYING TO COOL DOWN, BUT YOU'RE THE **ONLY ONE** WHO MANAGED TO!
THE END

# A Far-Too-Secret Secret!

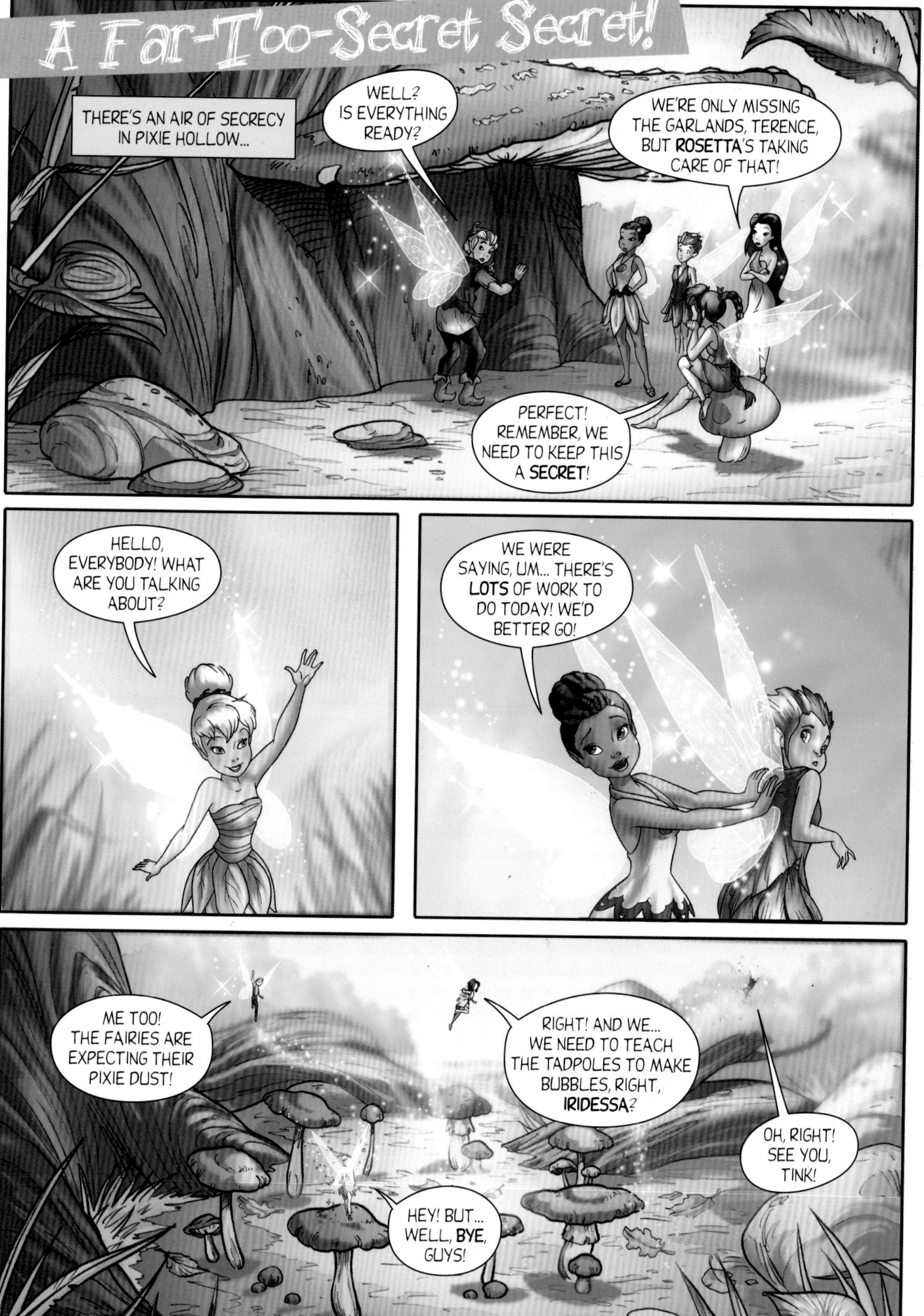

THERE'S AN AIR OF SECRECY IN PIXIE HOLLOW...
WELL? IS EVERYTHING READY?
WE'RE ONLY MISSING THE GARLANDS, TERENCE, BUT ROSETTA'S TAKING CARE OF THAT!
PERFECT! REMEMBER, WE NEED TO KEEP THIS A SECRET!
HELLO, EVERYBODY! WHAT ARE YOU TALKING ABOUT?
WE WERE SAYING, UM... THERE'S LOTS OF WORK TO DO TODAY! WE'D BETTER GO!
ME TOO! THE FAIRIES ARE EXPECTING THEIR PIXIE DUST!
RIGHT! AND WE... WE NEED TO TEACH THE TADPOLES TO MAKE BUBBLES, RIGHT, IRIDESSA?
OH, RIGHT! SEE YOU, TINK!
HEY! BUT... WELL, BYE, GUYS!

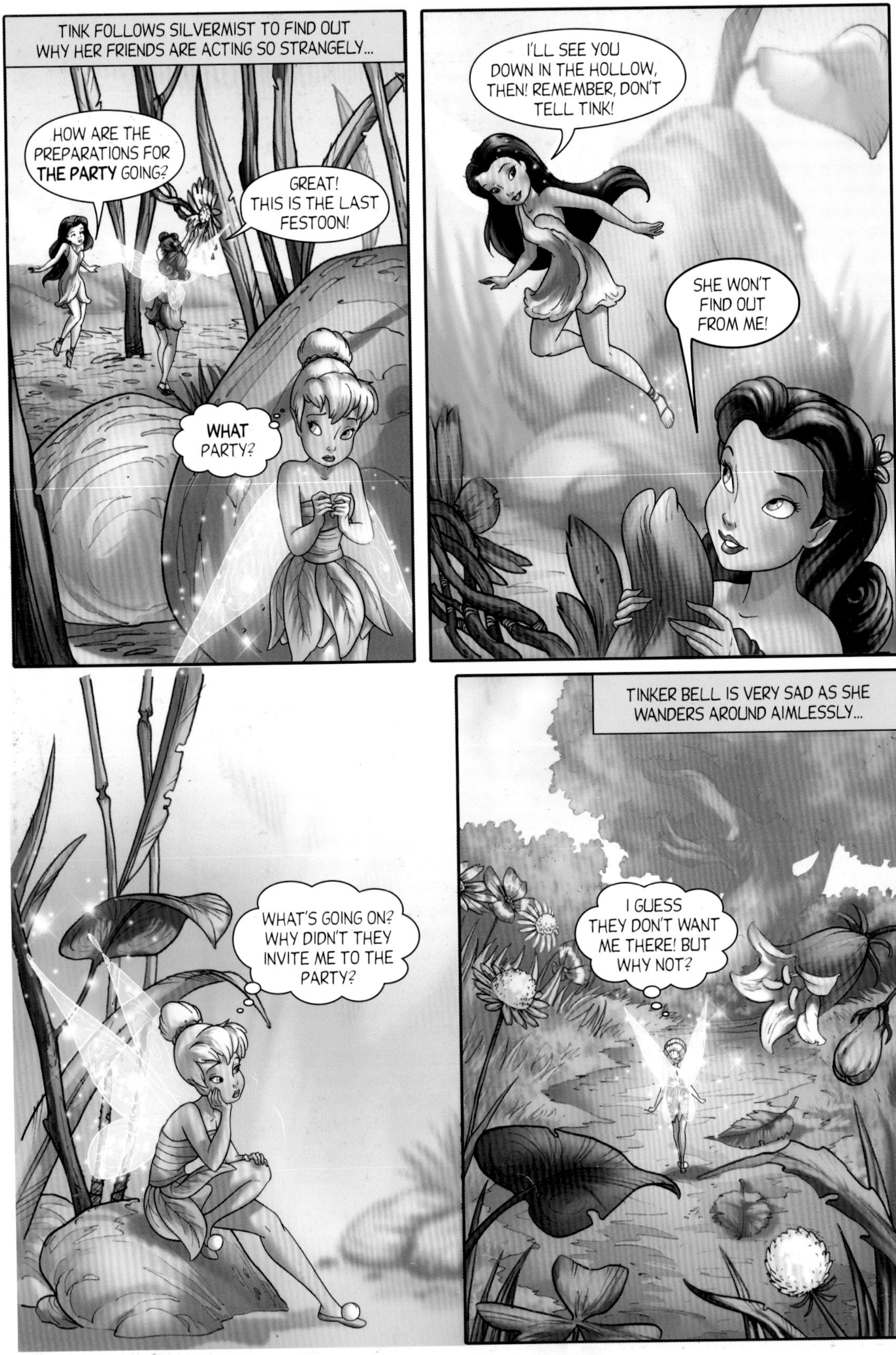
TINK FOLLOWS SILVERMIST TO FIND OUT WHY HER FRIENDS ARE ACTING SO STRANGELY...
HOW ARE THE PREPARATIONS FOR **THE PARTY** GOING?
GREAT! THIS IS THE LAST FESTOON!
**WHAT** PARTY?
I'LL SEE YOU DOWN IN THE HOLLOW, THEN! REMEMBER, DON'T TELL TINK!
SHE WON'T FIND OUT FROM ME!
WHAT'S GOING ON? WHY DIDN'T THEY INVITE ME TO THE PARTY?
TINKER BELL IS VERY SAD AS SHE WANDERS AROUND AIMLESSLY...
I GUESS THEY DON'T WANT ME THERE! BUT WHY NOT?

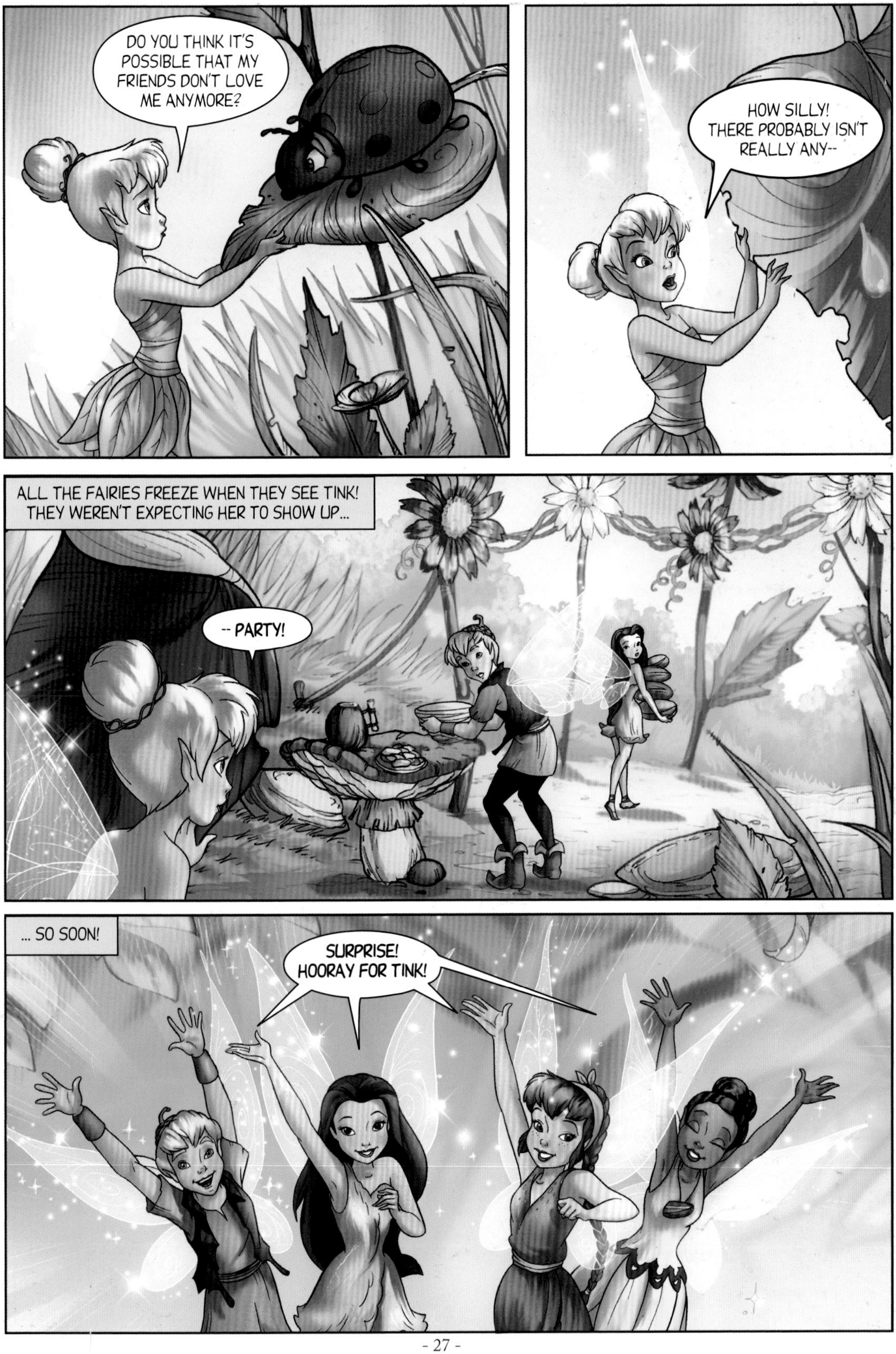
DO YOU THINK IT'S POSSIBLE THAT MY FRIENDS DON'T LOVE ME ANYMORE?
HOW SILLY! THERE PROBABLY ISN'T REALLY ANY--
ALL THE FAIRIES FREEZE WHEN THEY SEE TINK! THEY WEREN'T EXPECTING HER TO SHOW UP...
-- PARTY!
... SO SOON!
SURPRISE! HOORAY FOR TINK!

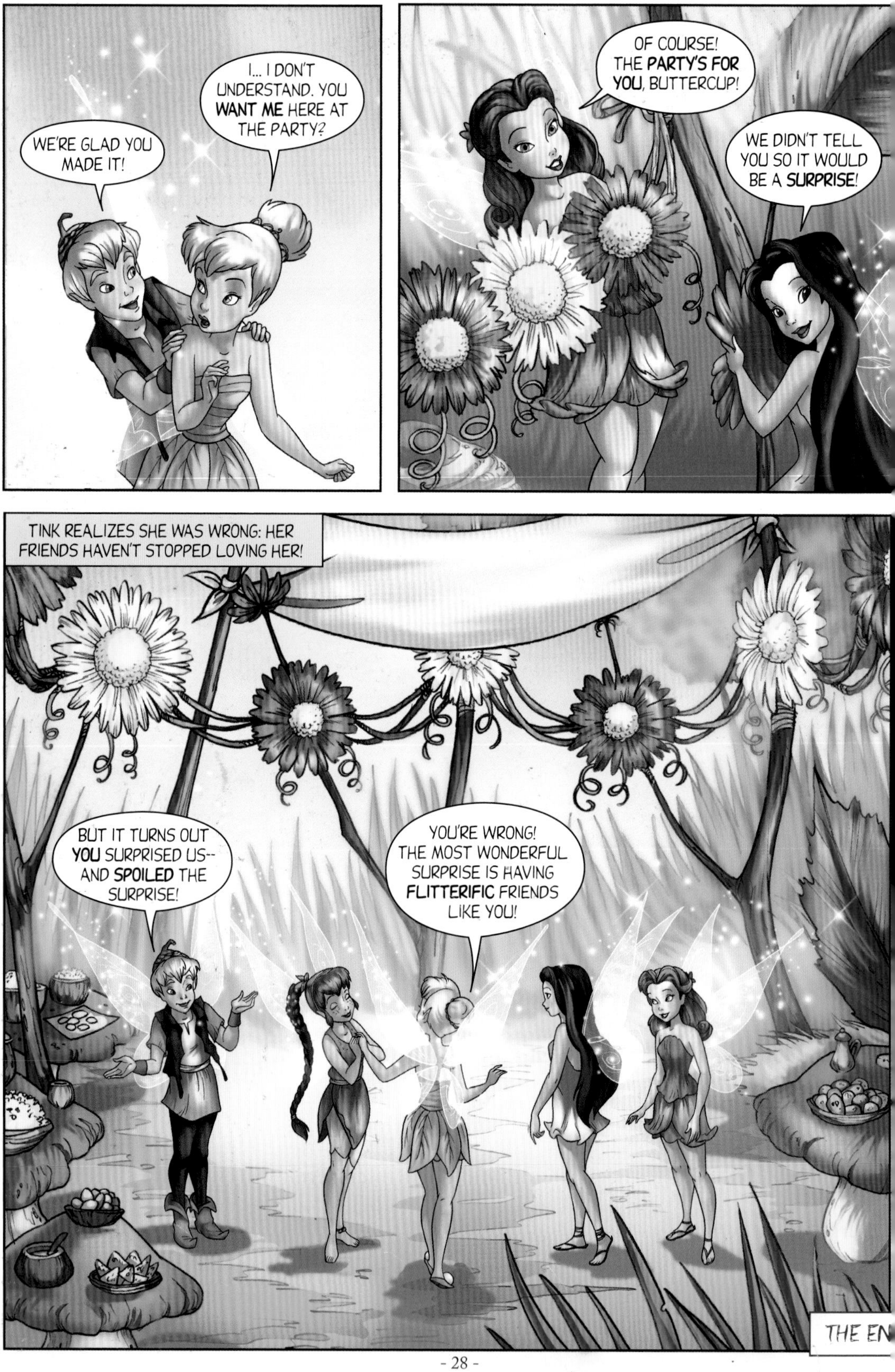
WE'RE GLAD YOU MADE IT!
I... I DON'T UNDERSTAND. YOU WANT ME HERE AT THE PARTY?
OF COURSE! THE PARTY'S FOR YOU, BUTTERCUP!
WE DIDN'T TELL YOU SO IT WOULD BE A SURPRISE!
TINK REALIZES SHE WAS WRONG: HER FRIENDS HAVEN'T STOPPED LOVING HER!
BUT IT TURNS OUT YOU SURPRISED US-- AND SPOILED THE SURPRISE!
YOU'RE WRONG! THE MOST WONDERFUL SURPRISE IS HAVING FLITTERIFIC FRIENDS LIKE YOU!
THE EN

# A Question of Taste!

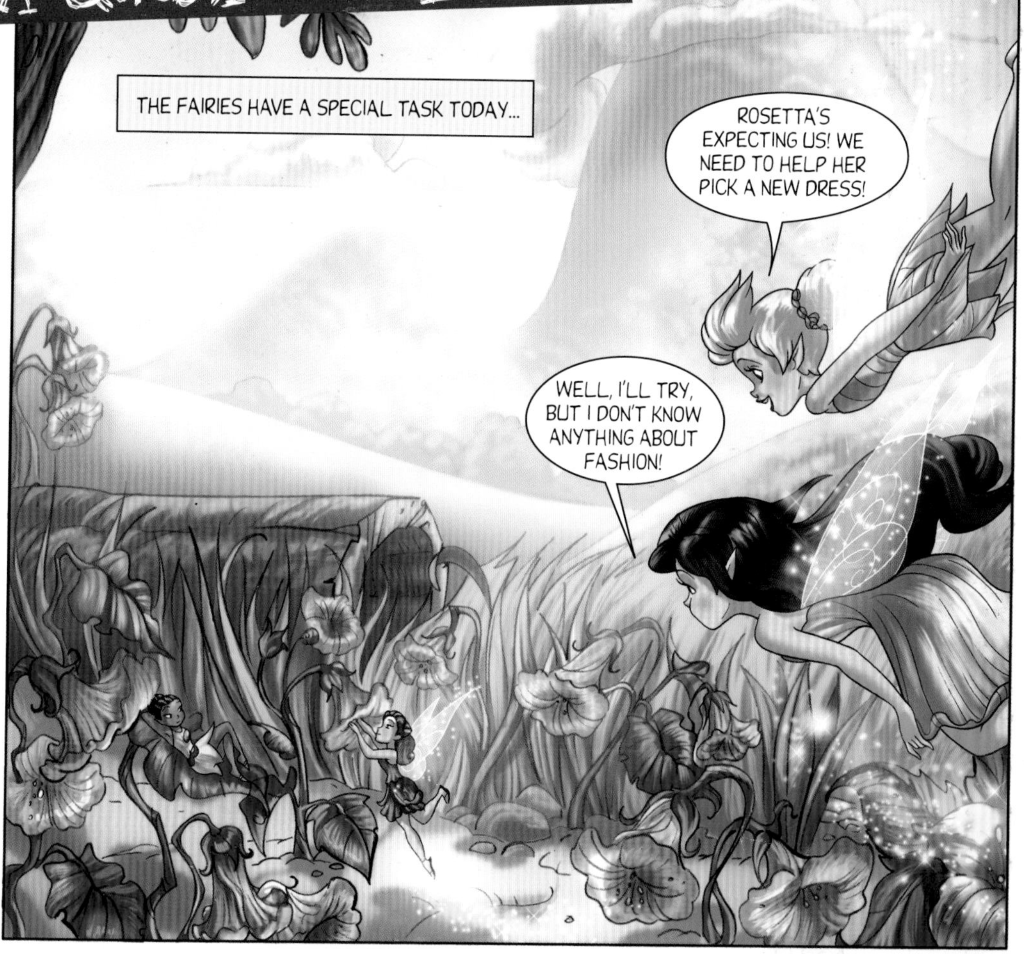
THE FAIRIES HAVE A SPECIAL TASK TODAY...
ROSETTA'S EXPECTING US! WE NEED TO HELP HER PICK A NEW DRESS!
WELL, I'LL TRY, BUT I DON'T KNOW ANYTHING ABOUT FASHION!

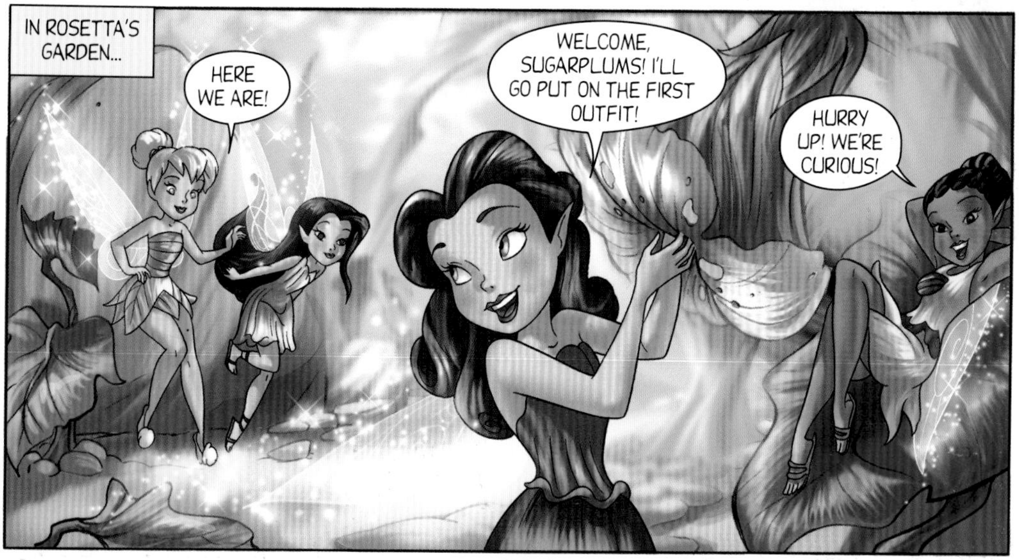
IN ROSETTA'S GARDEN...
HERE WE ARE!
WELCOME, SUGARPLUMS! I'LL GO PUT ON THE FIRST OUTFIT!
HURRY UP! WE'RE CURIOUS!

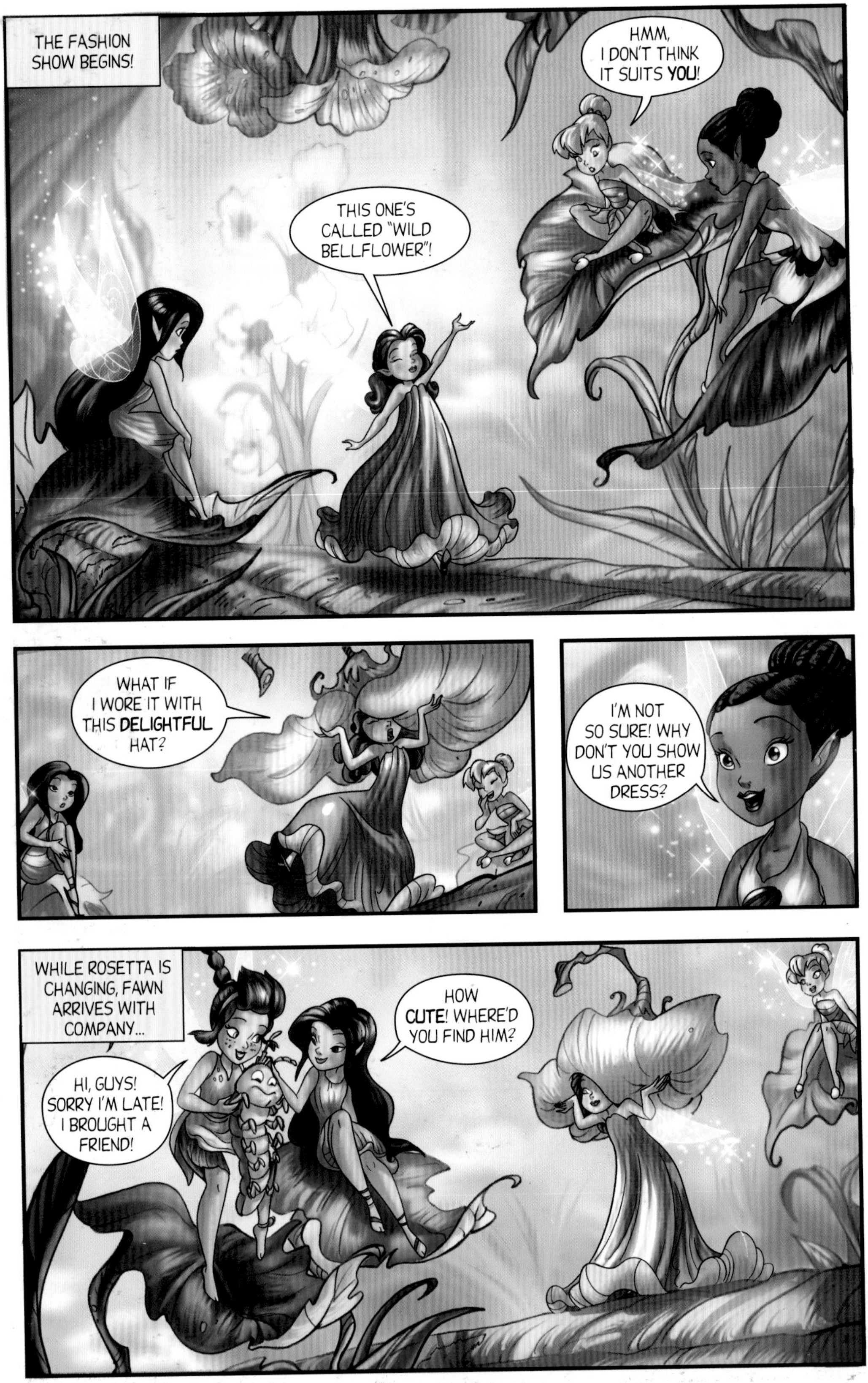
THE FASHION SHOW BEGINS!
HMM, I DON'T THINK IT SUITS **YOU**!
THIS ONE'S CALLED "WILD BELLFLOWER"!
WHAT IF I WORE IT WITH THIS **DELIGHTFUL** HAT?
I'M NOT SO SURE! WHY DON'T YOU SHOW US ANOTHER DRESS?
WHILE ROSETTA IS CHANGING, FAWN ARRIVES WITH COMPANY...
HI, GUYS! SORRY I'M LATE! I BROUGHT A FRIEND!
HOW **CUTE**! WHERE'D YOU FIND HIM?

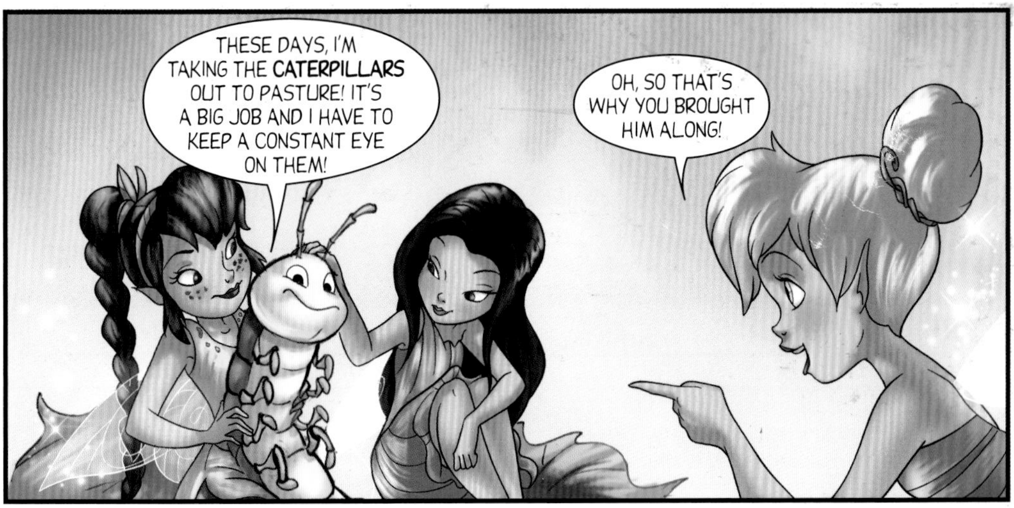
THESE DAYS, I'M TAKING THE **CATERPILLARS** OUT TO PASTURE! IT'S A BIG JOB AND I HAVE TO KEEP A CONSTANT EYE ON THEM!
OH, SO THAT'S WHY YOU BROUGHT HIM ALONG!

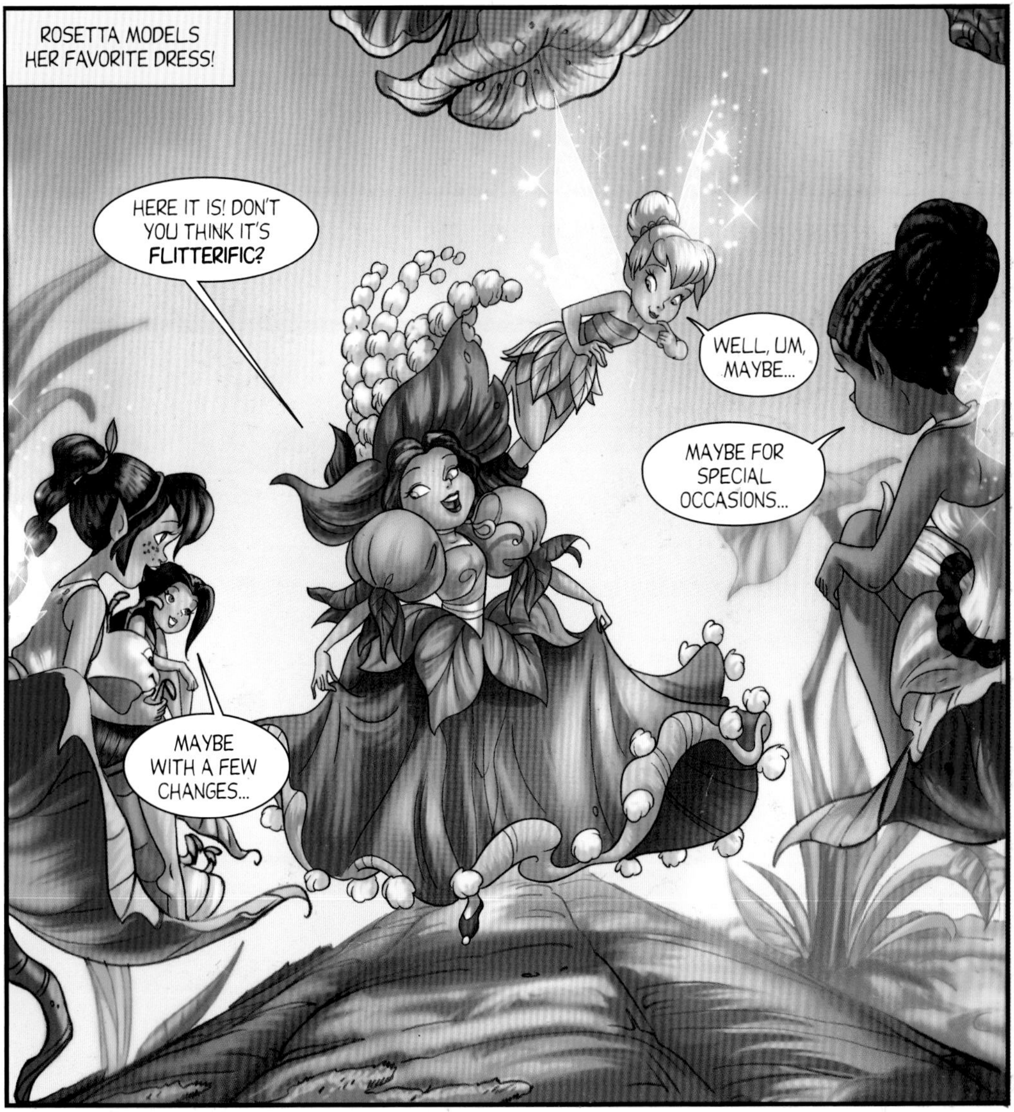
ROSETTA MODELS HER FAVORITE DRESS!
HERE IT IS! DON'T YOU THINK IT'S **FLITTERIFIC?**
WELL, UM, MAYBE...
MAYBE FOR SPECIAL OCCASIONS...
MAYBE WITH A FEW CHANGES...

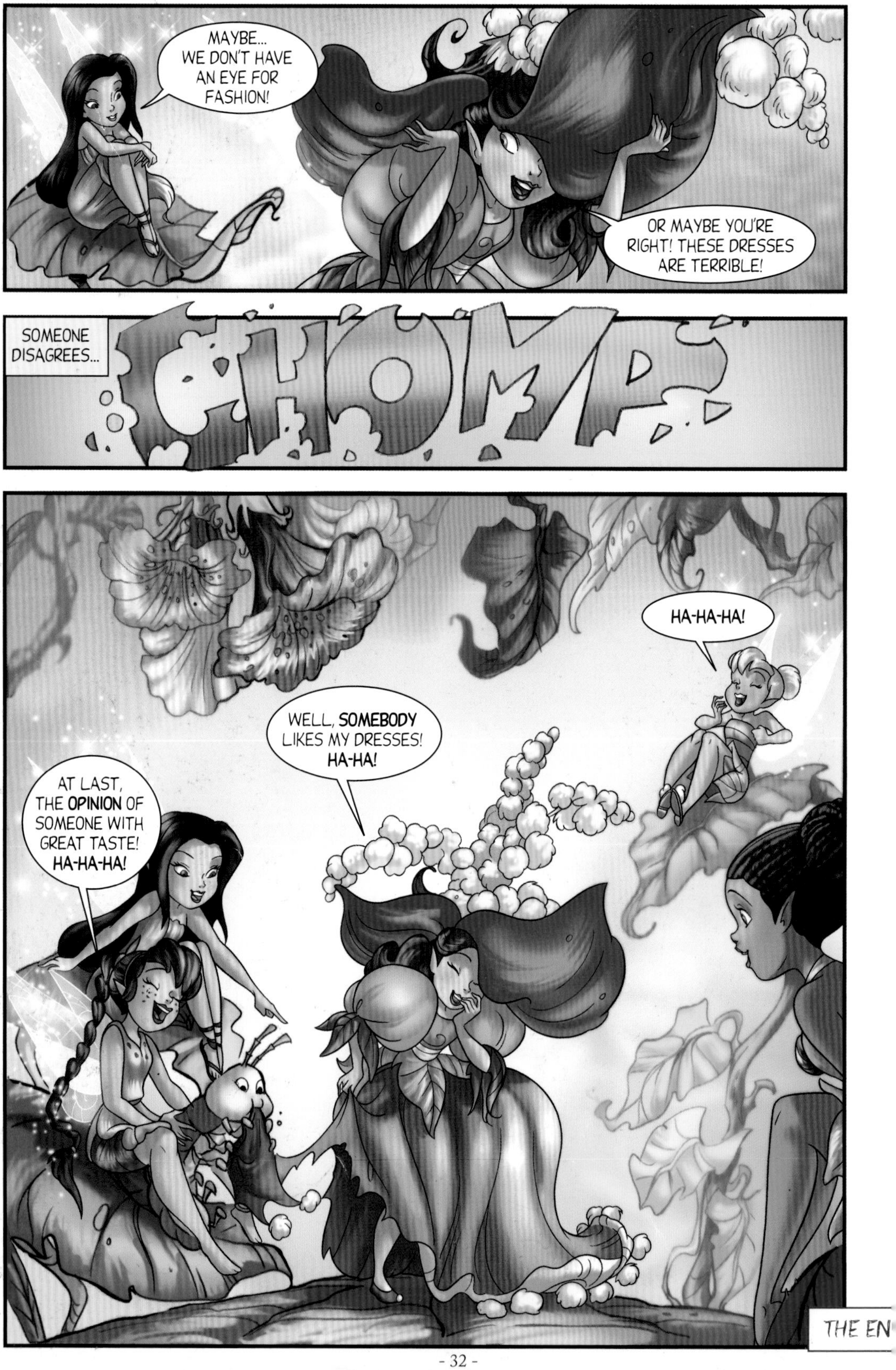
MAYBE... WE DON'T HAVE AN EYE FOR FASHION!
OR MAYBE YOU'RE RIGHT! THESE DRESSES ARE TERRIBLE!
SOMEONE DISAGREES...
CHOMP
HA-HA-HA!
WELL, SOMEBODY LIKES MY DRESSES! HA-HA!
AT LAST, THE OPINION OF SOMEONE WITH GREAT TASTE! HA-HA-HA!
THE EN

# One for All, All for One!

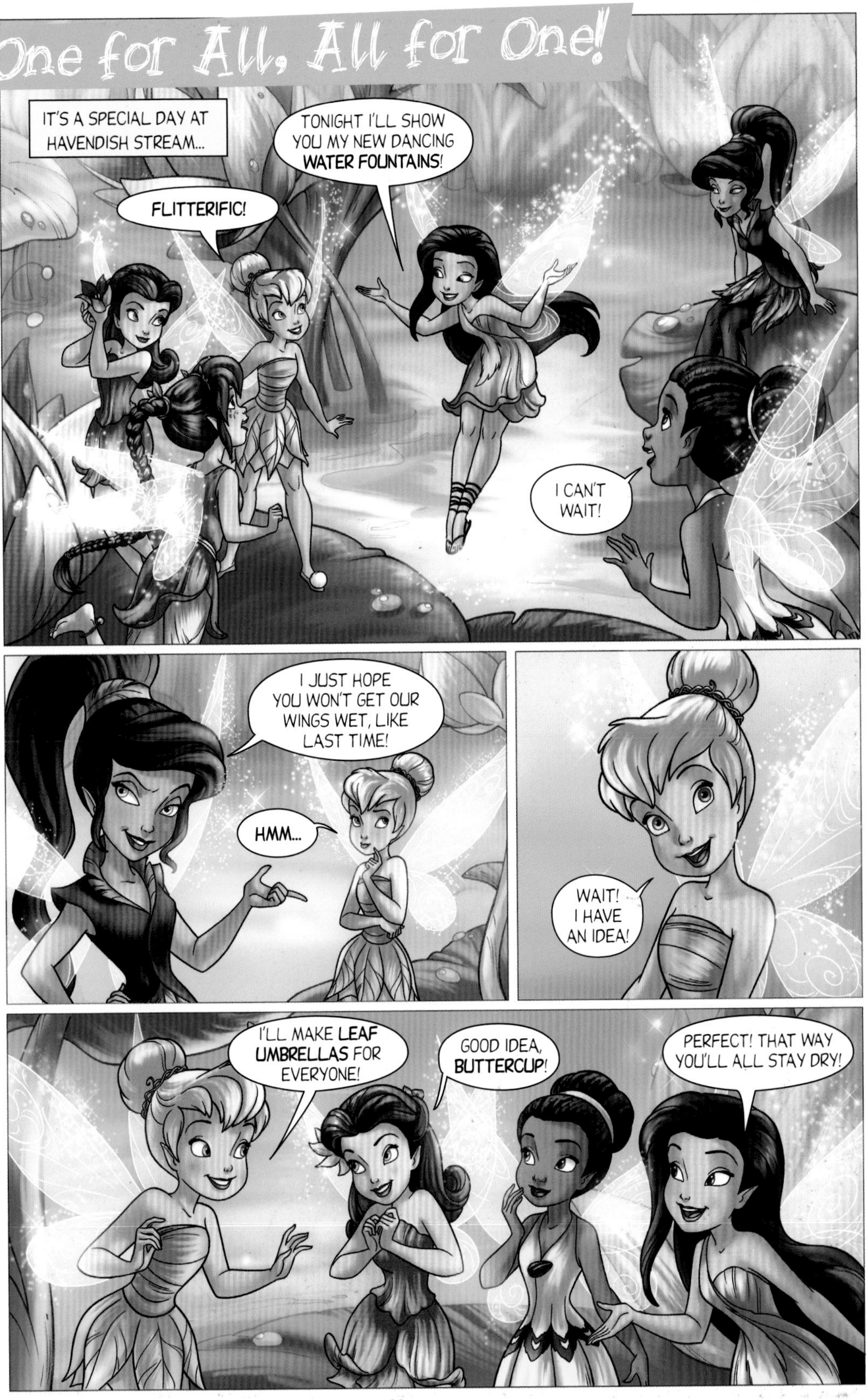

IT'S A SPECIAL DAY AT HAVENDISH STREAM...
TONIGHT I'LL SHOW YOU MY NEW DANCING **WATER FOUNTAINS**!
**FLITTERIFIC!**
I CAN'T WAIT!
I JUST HOPE YOU WON'T GET OUR WINGS WET, LIKE LAST TIME!
**HMM...**
WAIT! I HAVE AN IDEA!
I'LL MAKE **LEAF UMBRELLAS** FOR EVERYONE!
GOOD IDEA, **BUTTERCUP**!
PERFECT! THAT WAY YOU'LL ALL STAY DRY!

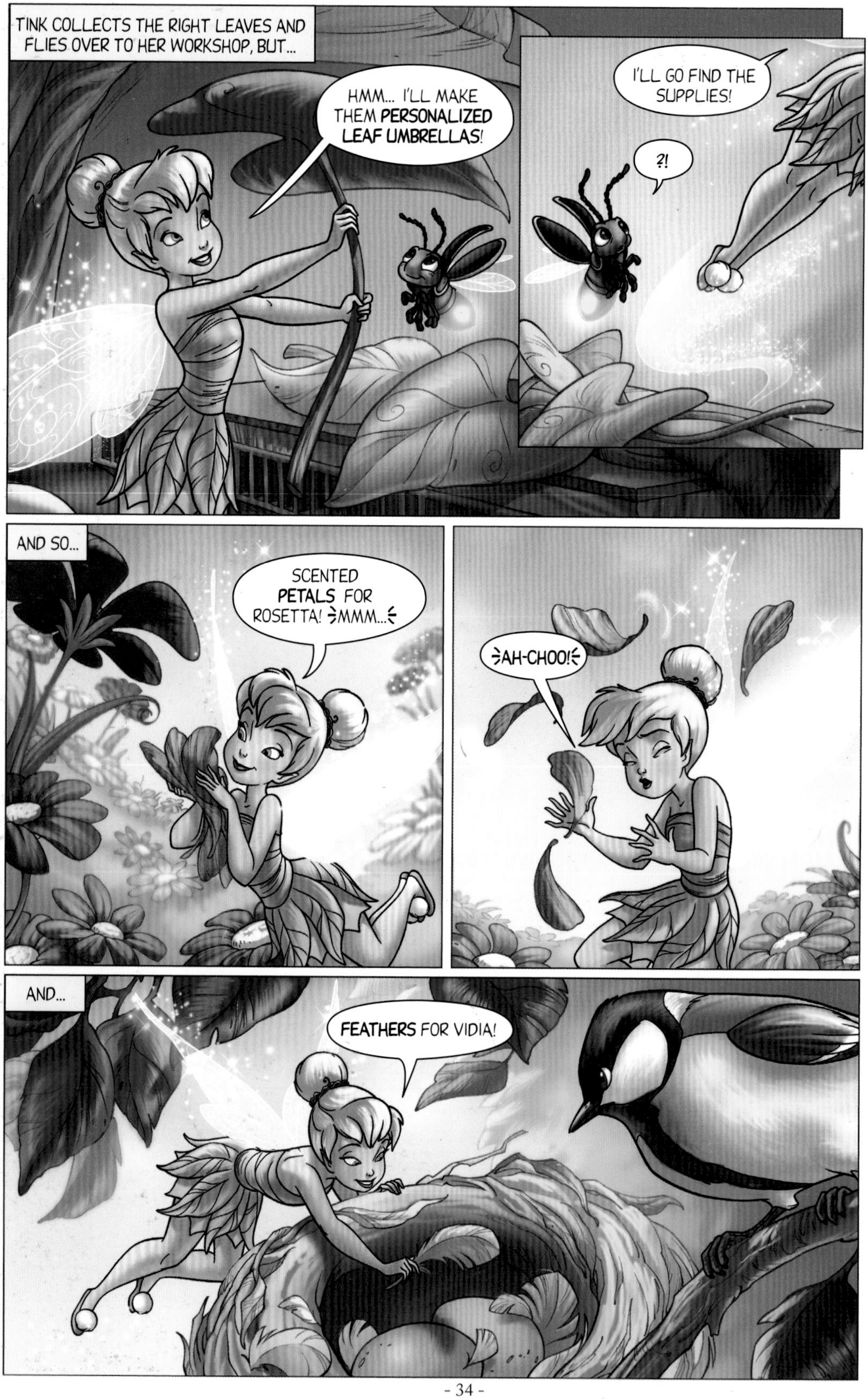
TINK COLLECTS THE RIGHT LEAVES AND FLIES OVER TO HER WORKSHOP, BUT...
HMM... I'LL MAKE THEM **PERSONALIZED LEAF UMBRELLAS**!
I'LL GO FIND THE SUPPLIES!
?!
AND SO...
SCENTED **PETALS** FOR ROSETTA! MMM...
AH-CHOO!
AND...
**FEATHERS** FOR VIDIA!

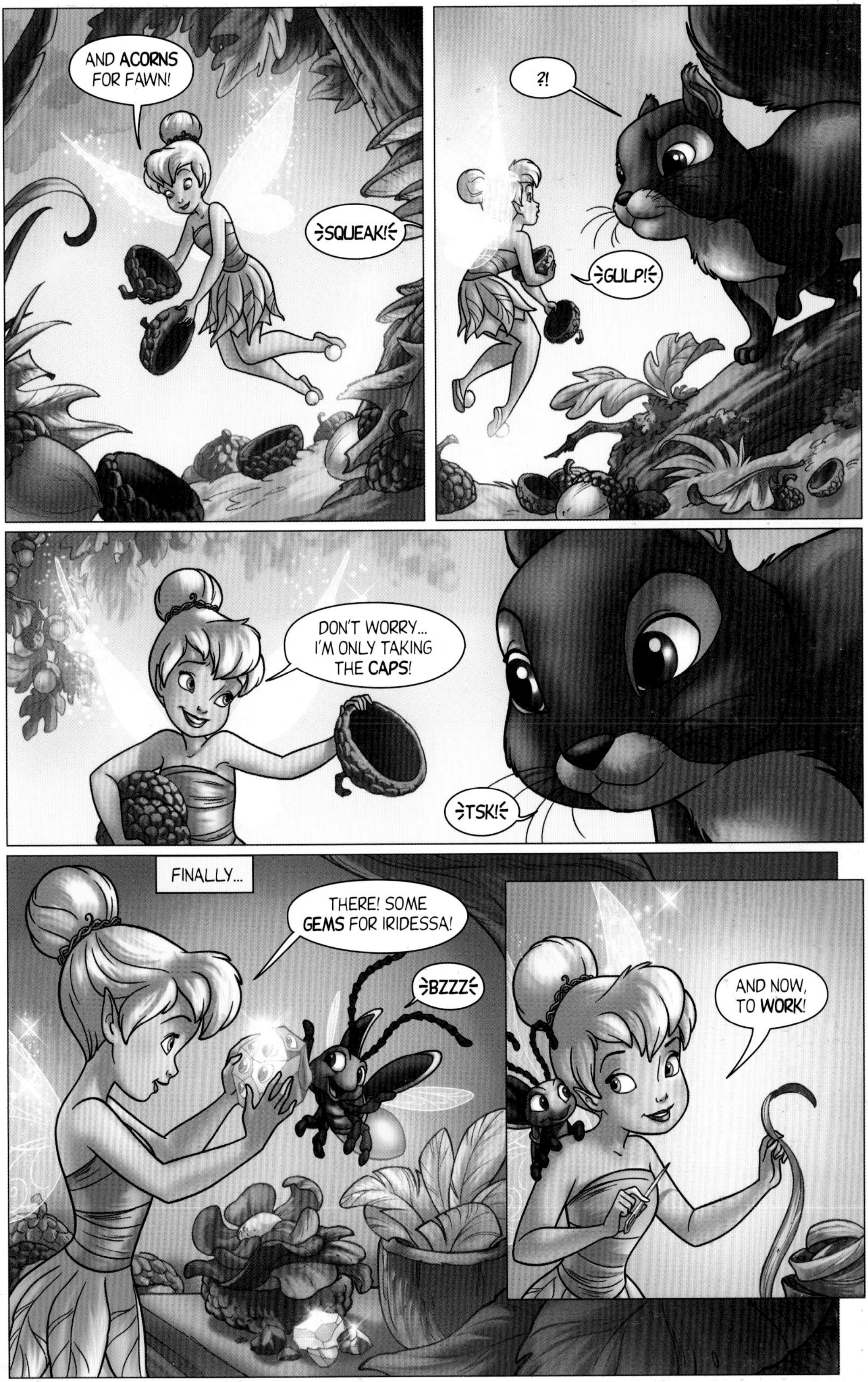
AND ACORNS FOR FAWN!
SQUEAK!
?!
GULP!
DON'T WORRY... I'M ONLY TAKING THE CAPS!
TSK!
FINALLY...
THERE! SOME GEMS FOR IRIDESSA!
BZZZ
AND NOW, TO WORK!

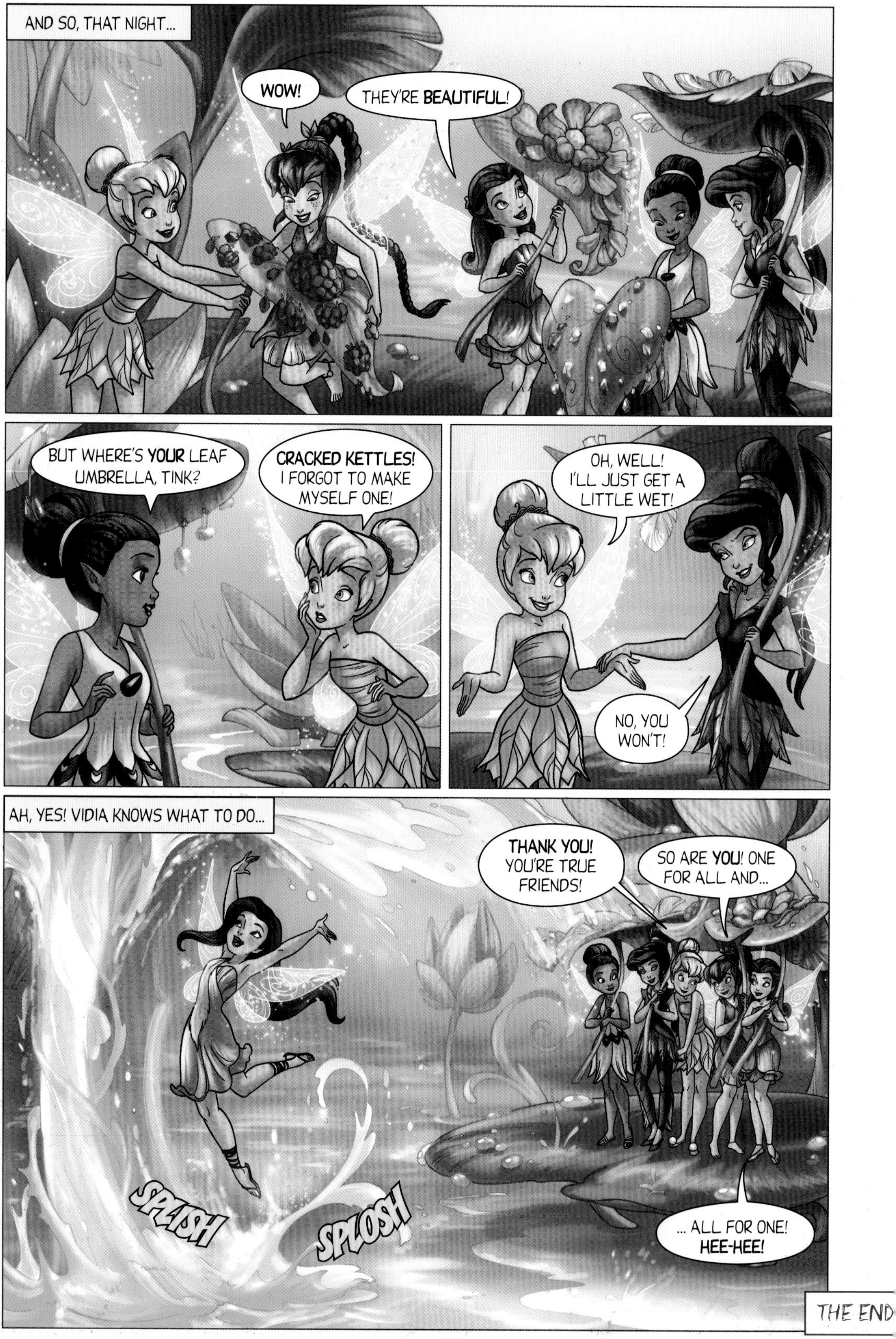

AND SO, THAT NIGHT...
WOW!
THEY'RE BEAUTIFUL!
BUT WHERE'S YOUR LEAF UMBRELLA, TINK?
CRACKED KETTLES! I FORGOT TO MAKE MYSELF ONE!
OH, WELL! I'LL JUST GET A LITTLE WET!
NO, YOU WON'T!
AH, YES! VIDIA KNOWS WHAT TO DO...
SPLISH
SPLOSH
THANK YOU! YOU'RE TRUE FRIENDS!
SO ARE YOU! ONE FOR ALL AND...
... ALL FOR ONE! HEE-HEE!
THE END

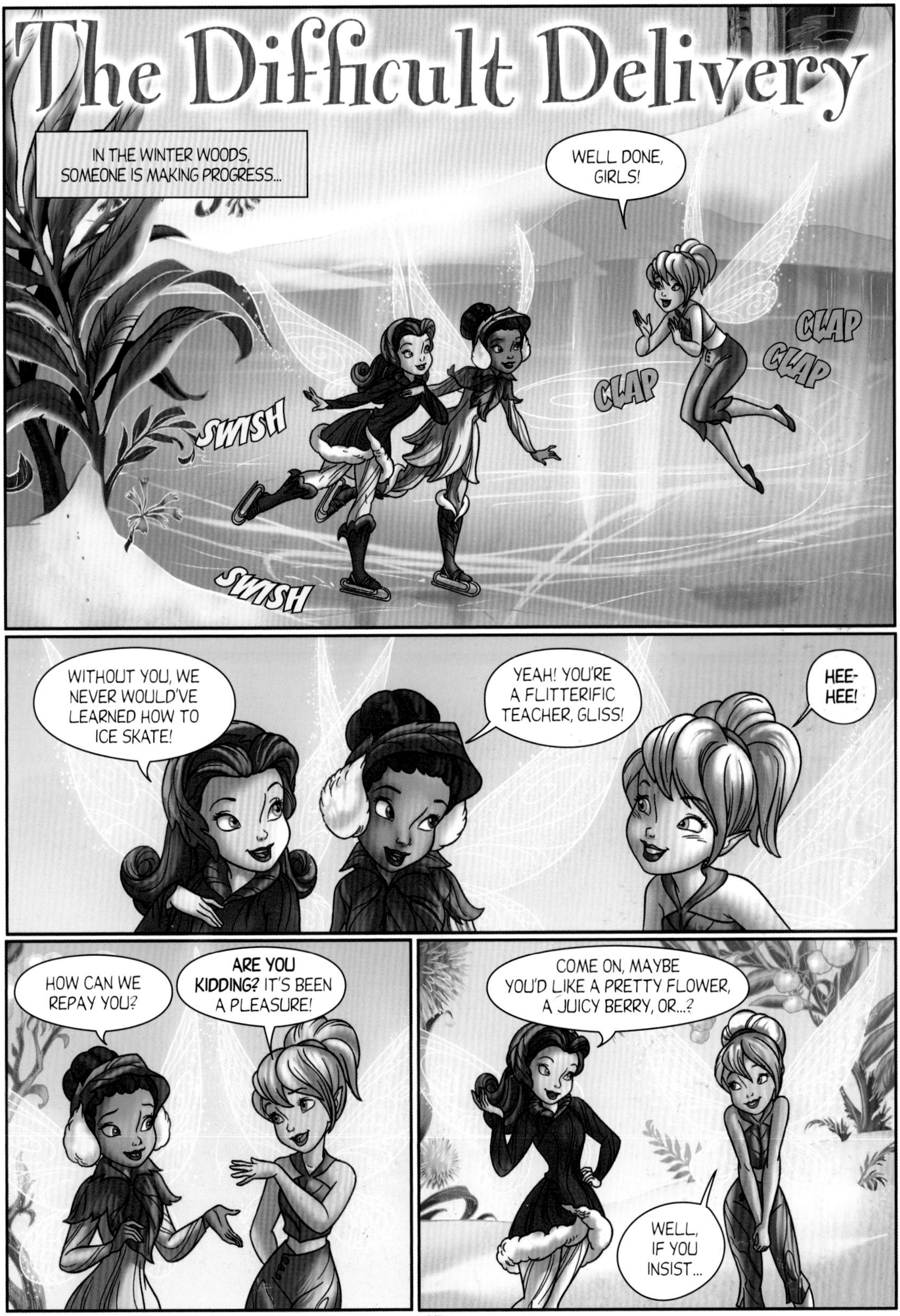

The Difficult Delivery
IN THE WINTER WOODS, SOMEONE IS MAKING PROGRESS...
WELL DONE, GIRLS!
CLAP
CLAP
CLAP
SWISH
SWISH
WITHOUT YOU, WE NEVER WOULD'VE LEARNED HOW TO ICE SKATE!
YEAH! YOU'RE A FLITTERIFIC TEACHER, GLISS!
HEE-HEE!
HOW CAN WE REPAY YOU?
ARE YOU KIDDING? IT'S BEEN A PLEASURE!
COME ON, MAYBE YOU'D LIKE A PRETTY FLOWER, A JUICY BERRY, OR...?
WELL, IF YOU INSIST...

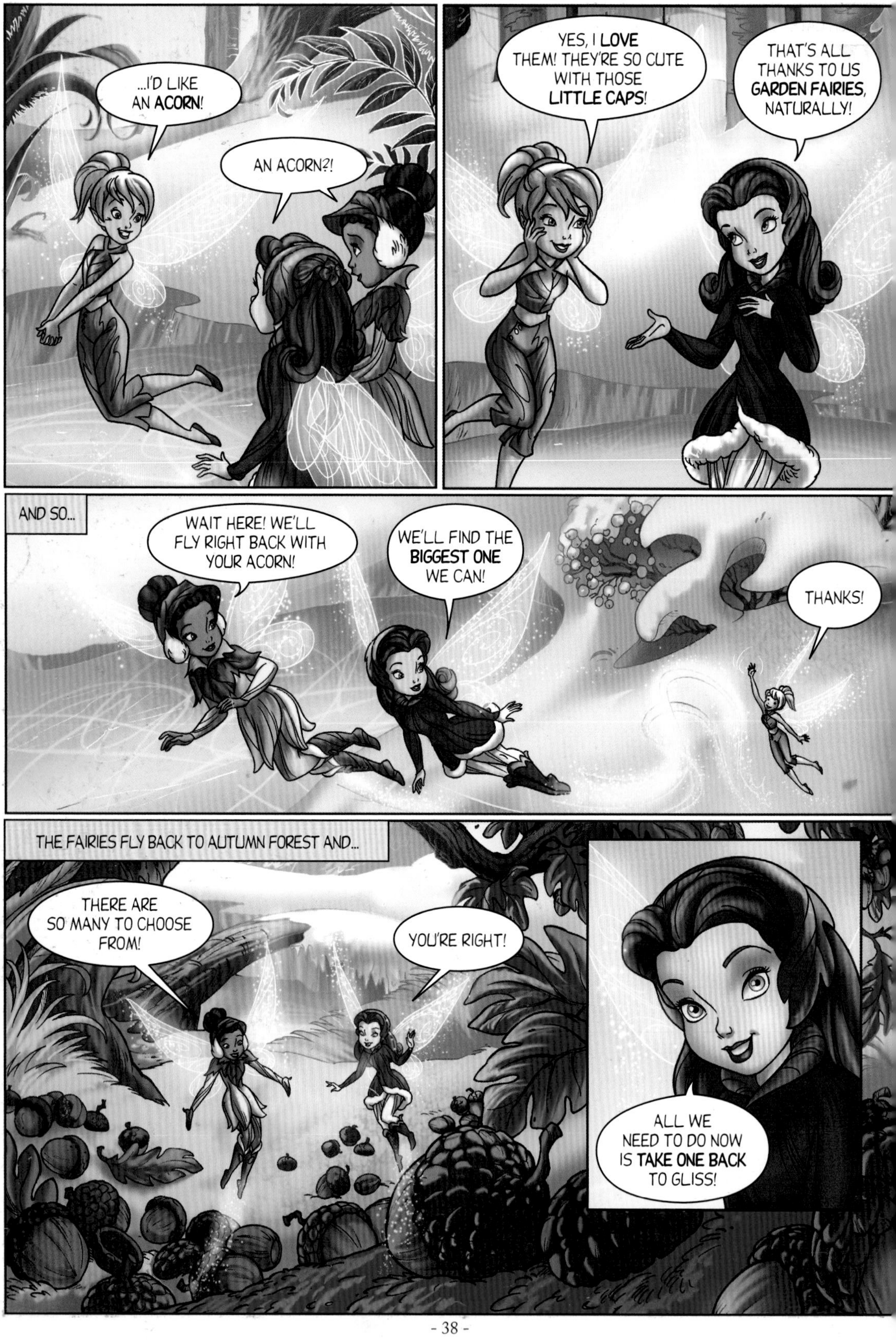
...I'D LIKE AN ACORN!
AN ACORN?!
YES, I LOVE THEM! THEY'RE SO CUTE WITH THOSE LITTLE CAPS!
THAT'S ALL THANKS TO US GARDEN FAIRIES, NATURALLY!
AND SO...
WAIT HERE! WE'LL FLY RIGHT BACK WITH YOUR ACORN!
WE'LL FIND THE BIGGEST ONE WE CAN!
THANKS!
THE FAIRIES FLY BACK TO AUTUMN FOREST AND...
THERE ARE SO MANY TO CHOOSE FROM!
YOU'RE RIGHT!
ALL WE NEED TO DO NOW IS TAKE ONE BACK TO GLISS!

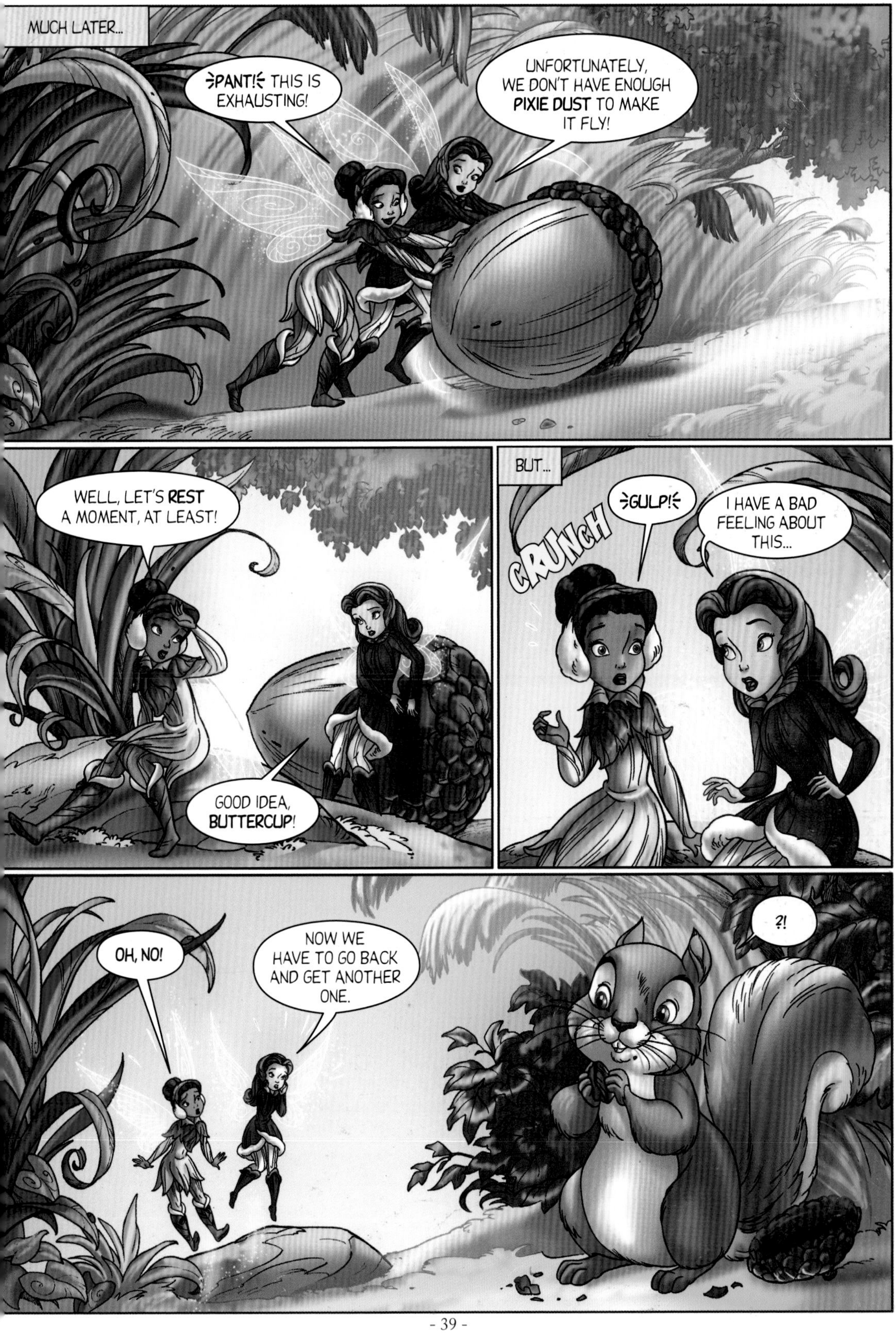
MUCH LATER...
PANT! THIS IS EXHAUSTING!
UNFORTUNATELY, WE DON'T HAVE ENOUGH PIXIE DUST TO MAKE IT FLY!
WELL, LET'S REST A MOMENT, AT LEAST!
GOOD IDEA, BUTTERCUP!
BUT...
CRUNCH
GULP!
I HAVE A BAD FEELING ABOUT THIS...
OH, NO!
NOW WE HAVE TO GO BACK AND GET ANOTHER ONE.
?!

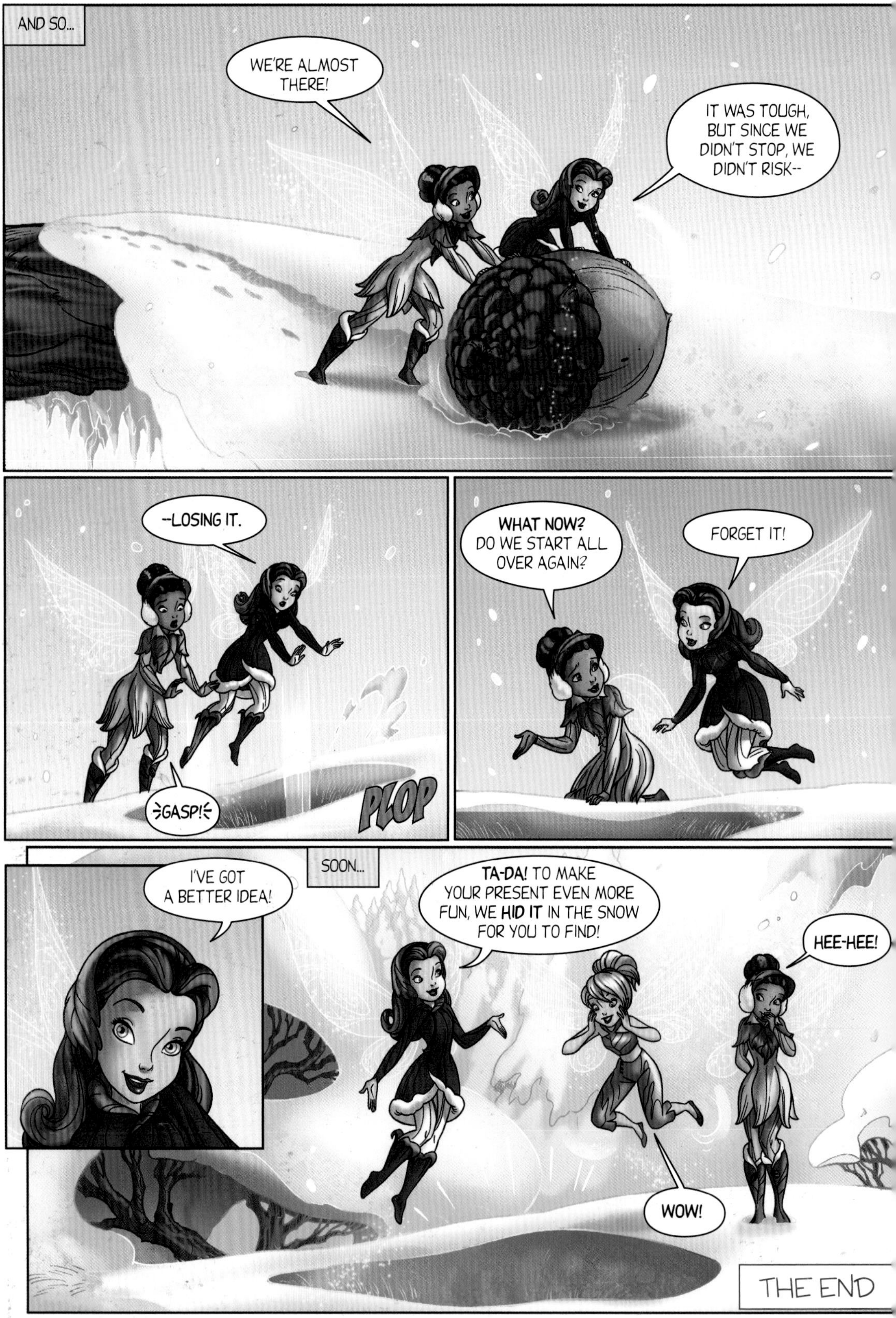
AND SO...
WE'RE ALMOST THERE!
IT WAS TOUGH, BUT SINCE WE DIDN'T STOP, WE DIDN'T RISK--
--LOSING IT.
GASP!
PLOP
WHAT NOW? DO WE START ALL OVER AGAIN?
FORGET IT!
I'VE GOT A BETTER IDEA!
SOON...
TA-DA! TO MAKE YOUR PRESENT EVEN MORE FUN, WE HID IT IN THE SNOW FOR YOU TO FIND!
HEE-HEE!
WOW!
THE END

# Mushroom Mayhem

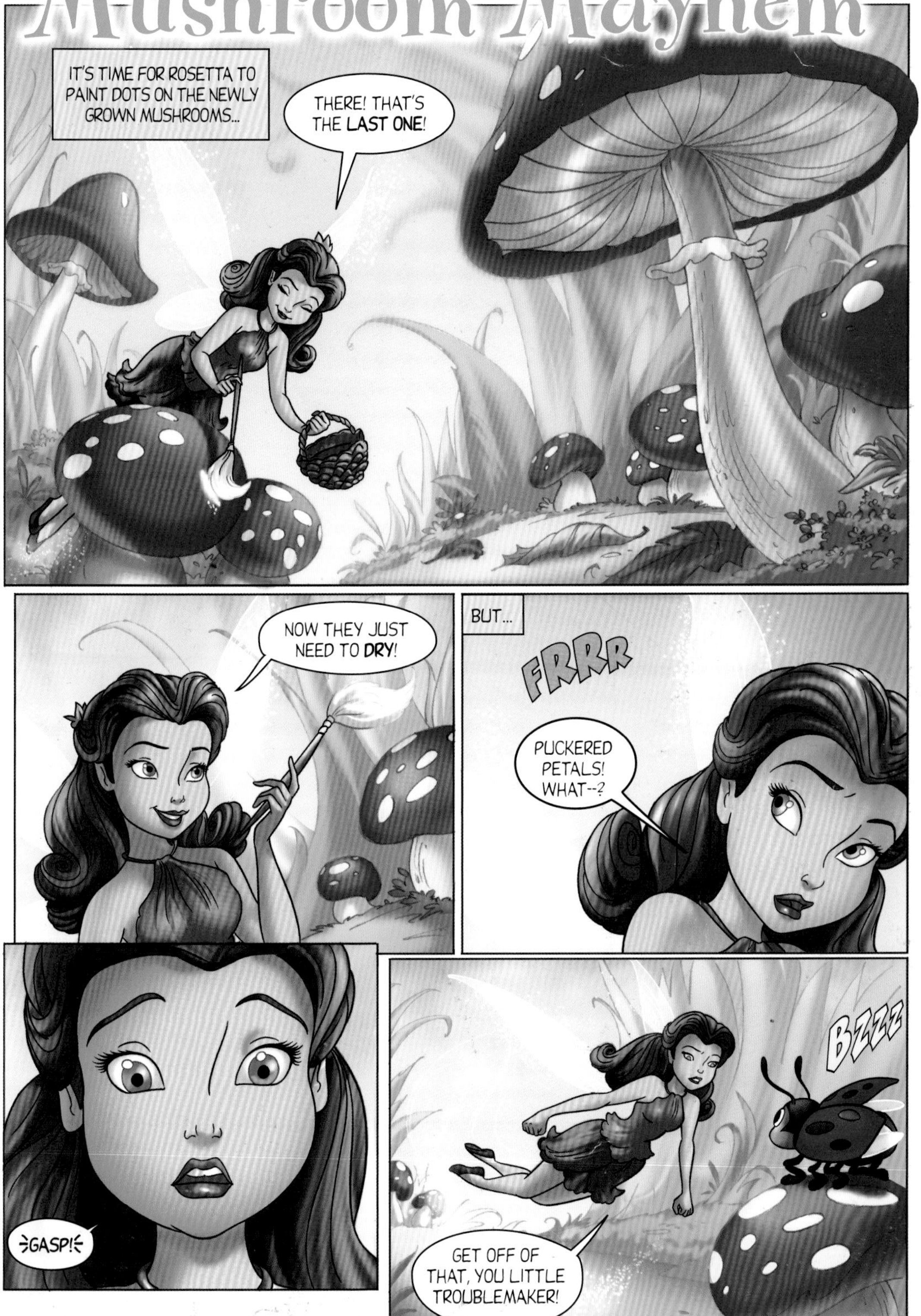
IT'S TIME FOR ROSETTA TO PAINT DOTS ON THE NEWLY GROWN MUSHROOMS...
THERE! THAT'S THE **LAST ONE**!
NOW THEY JUST NEED TO **DRY**!
BUT...
FRRR
PUCKERED PETALS! WHAT--?
GASP!
BZZZ
GET OFF OF THAT, YOU LITTLE TROUBLEMAKER!

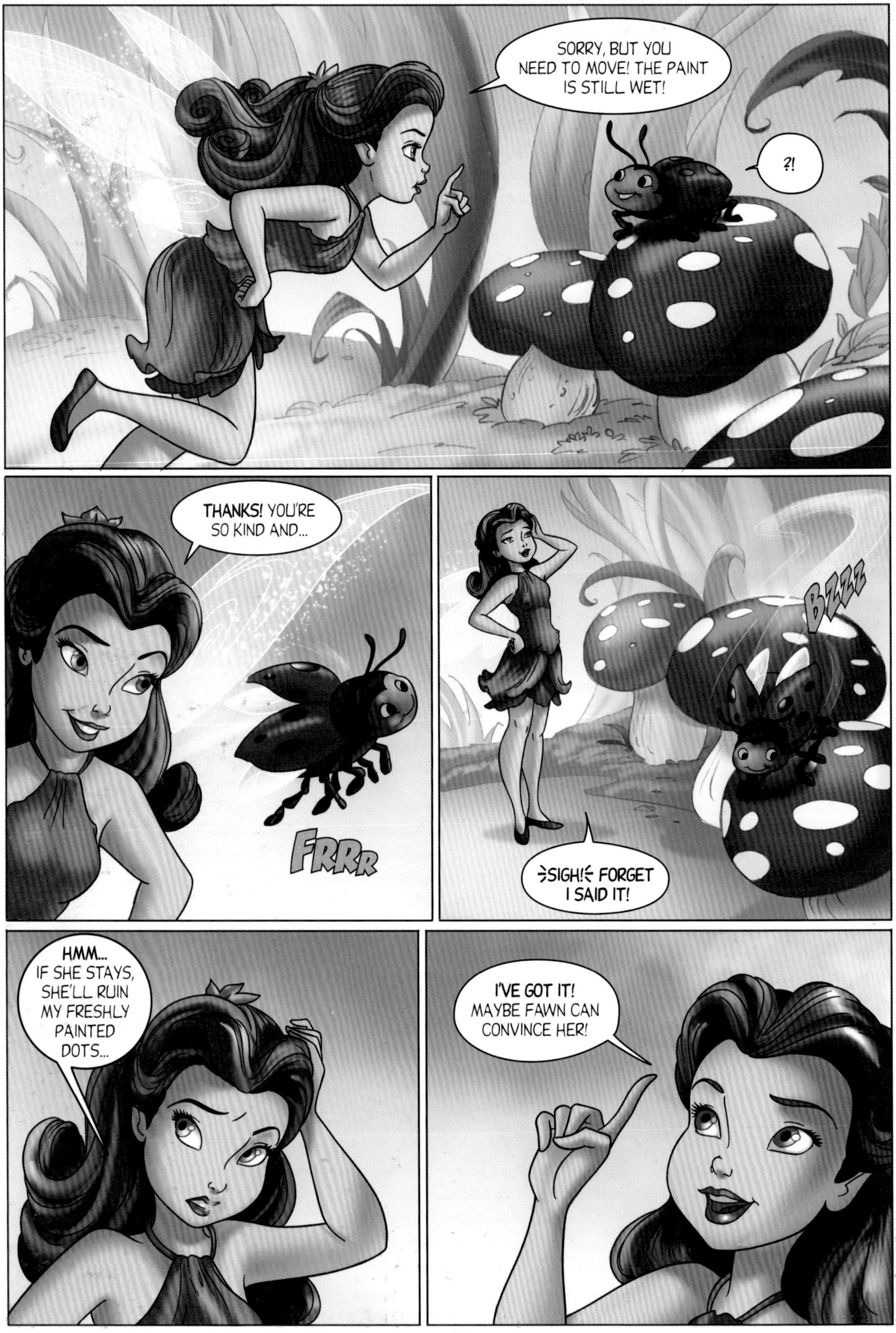
SORRY, BUT YOU NEED TO MOVE! THE PAINT IS STILL WET!
?!
THANKS! YOU'RE SO KIND AND...
FRRR
BZZZ
≑SIGH!≑ FORGET I SAID IT!
HMM... IF SHE STAYS, SHE'LL RUIN MY FRESHLY PAINTED DOTS...
I'VE GOT IT! MAYBE FAWN CAN CONVINCE HER!

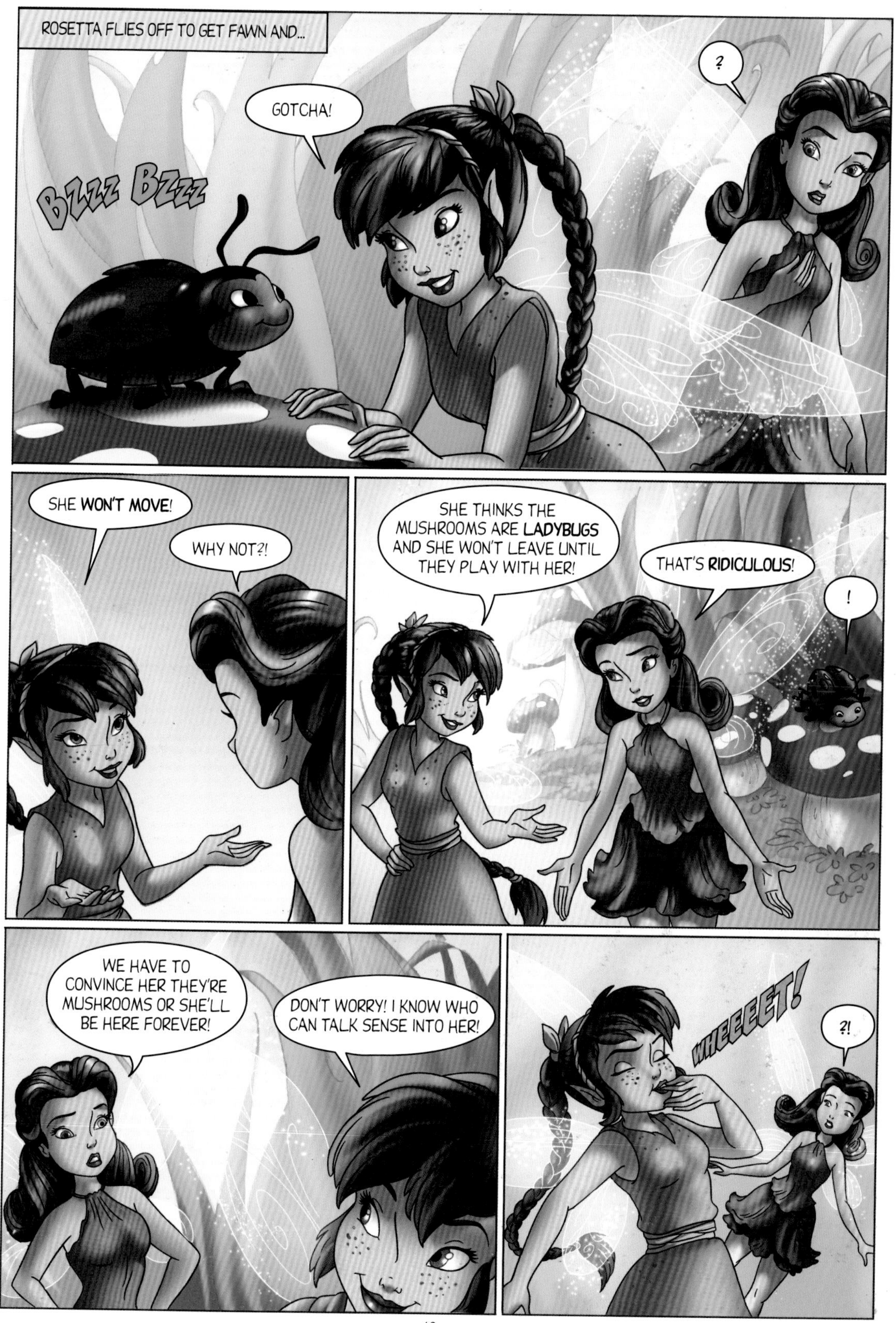
ROSETTA FLIES OFF TO GET FAWN AND...
BZZZ BZZZ
GOTCHA!
?
SHE WON'T MOVE!
WHY NOT?!
SHE THINKS THE MUSHROOMS ARE LADYBUGS AND SHE WON'T LEAVE UNTIL THEY PLAY WITH HER!
THAT'S RIDICULOUS!
!
WE HAVE TO CONVINCE HER THEY'RE MUSHROOMS OR SHE'LL BE HERE FOREVER!
DON'T WORRY! I KNOW WHO CAN TALK SENSE INTO HER!
WHEEEET!
?!

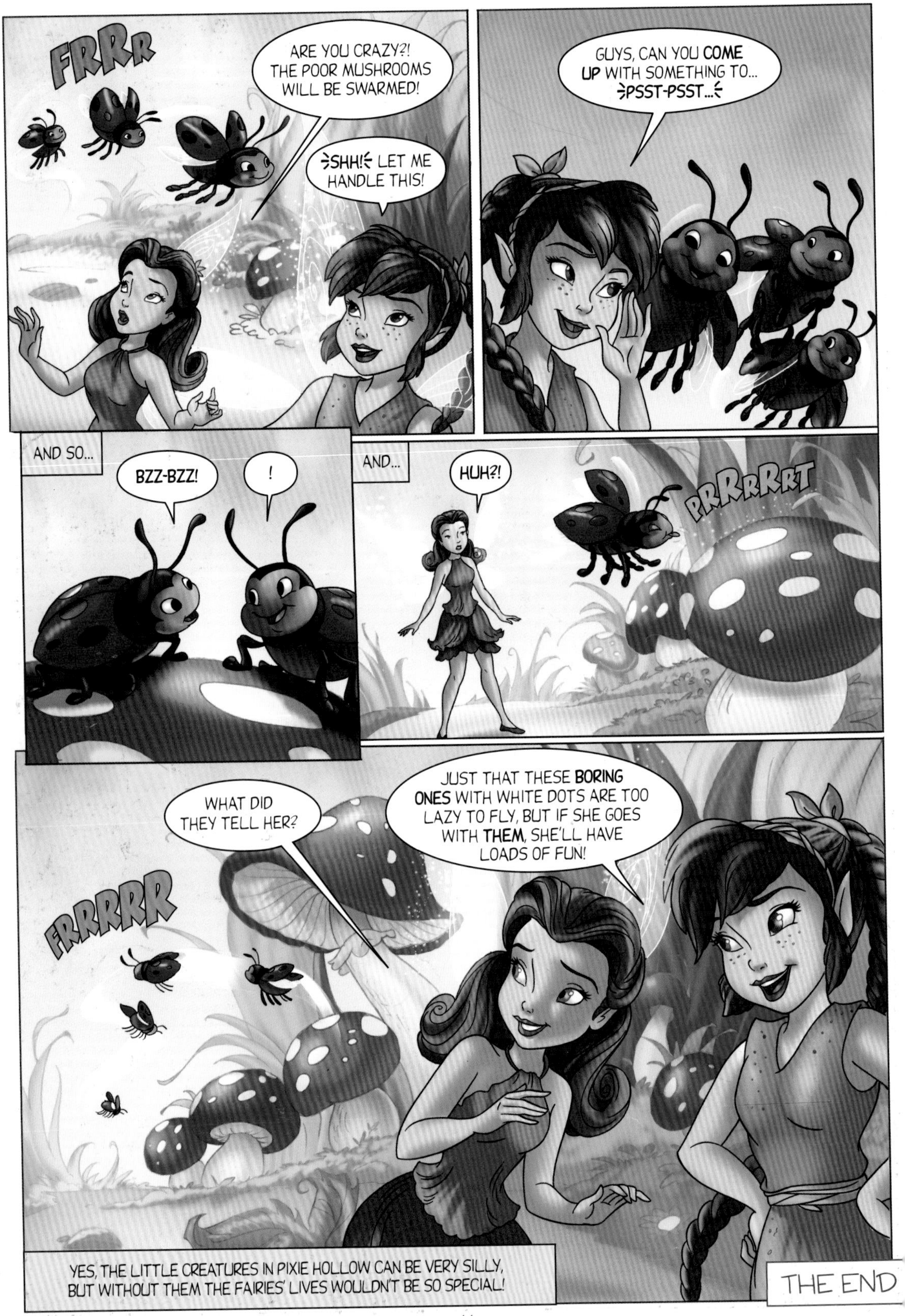
FRRR
ARE YOU CRAZY?! THE POOR MUSHROOMS WILL BE SWARMED!
SHH! LET ME HANDLE THIS!
GUYS, CAN YOU COME UP WITH SOMETHING TO... PSST-PSST...
AND SO...
BZZ-BZZ!
!
AND...
HUH?!
PRRRRRT
WHAT DID THEY TELL HER?
JUST THAT THESE BORING ONES WITH WHITE DOTS ARE TOO LAZY TO FLY, BUT IF SHE GOES WITH THEM, SHE'LL HAVE LOADS OF FUN!
FRRRRR
YES, THE LITTLE CREATURES IN PIXIE HOLLOW CAN BE VERY SILLY, BUT WITHOUT THEM THE FAIRIES' LIVES WOULDN'T BE SO SPECIAL!
THE END

# Perfumed and Perfect

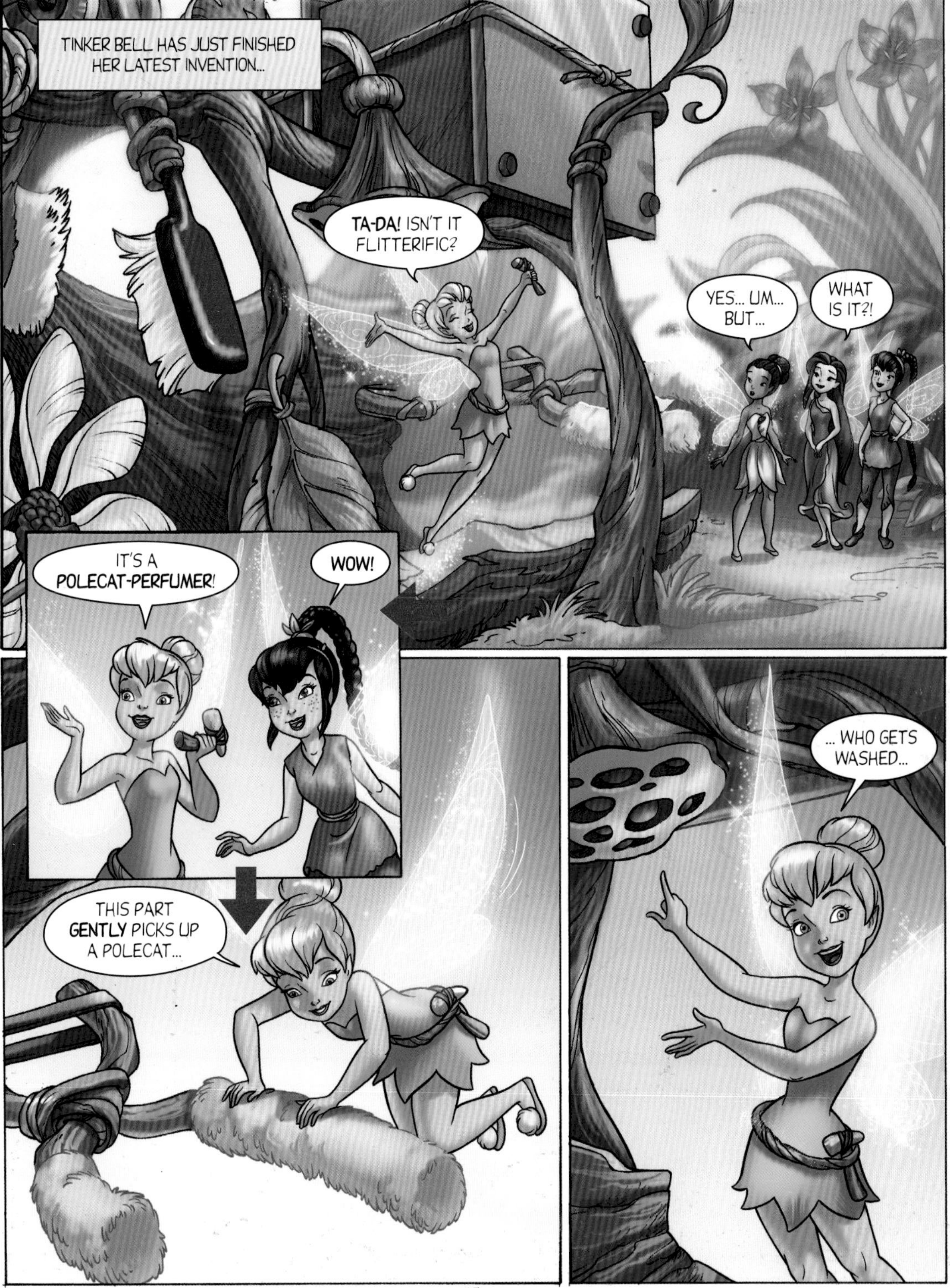

TINKER BELL HAS JUST FINISHED HER LATEST INVENTION...
TA-DA! ISN'T IT FLITTERIFIC?
YES... UM... BUT...
WHAT IS IT?!
IT'S A POLECAT-PERFUMER!
WOW!
THIS PART GENTLY PICKS UP A POLECAT...
... WHO GETS WASHED...

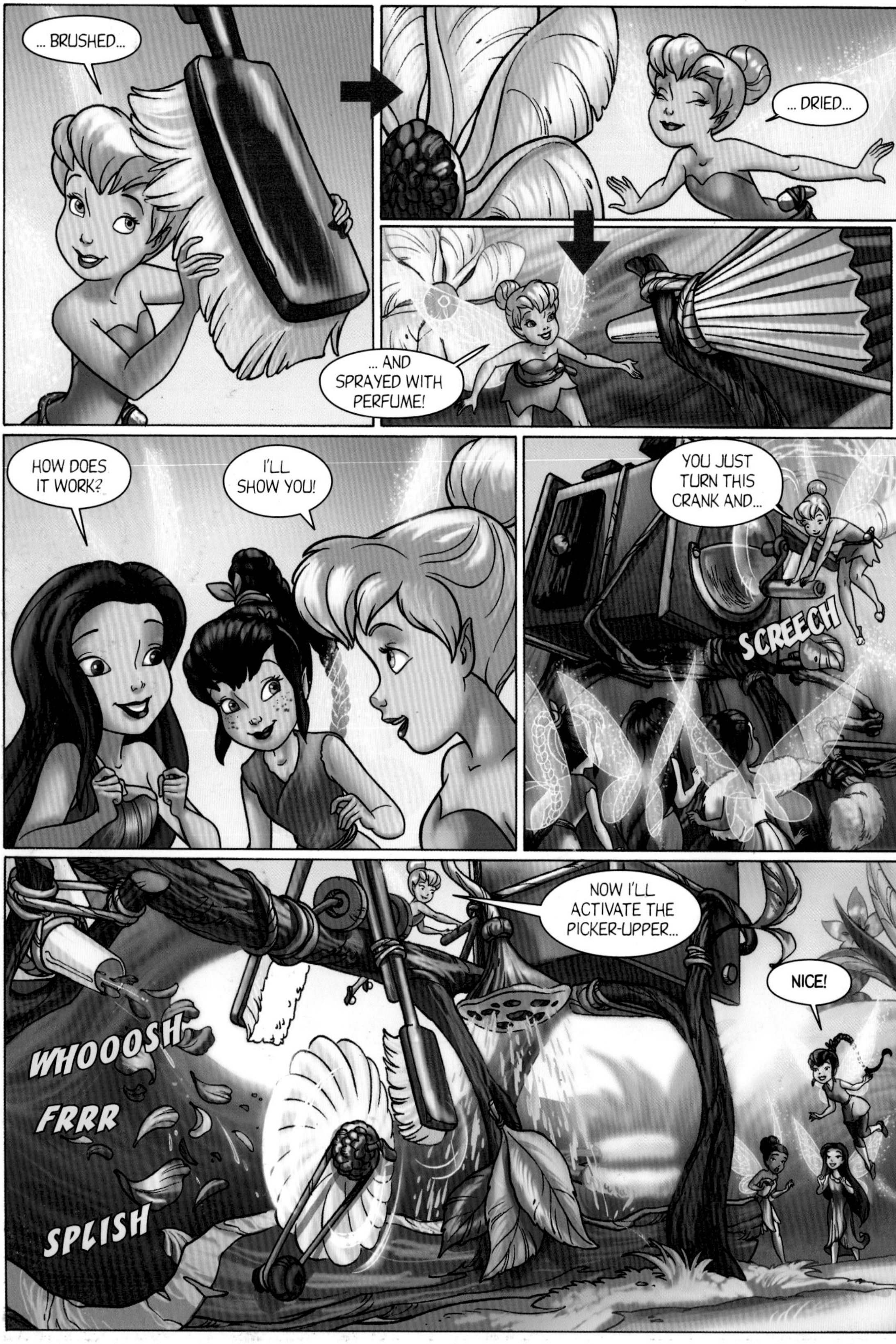
... BRUSHED...
... DRIED...
... AND SPRAYED WITH PERFUME!
HOW DOES IT WORK?
I'LL SHOW YOU!
YOU JUST TURN THIS CRANK AND...
SCREECH
NOW I'LL ACTIVATE THE PICKER-UPPER...
NICE!
WHOOOSH
FRRR
SPLISH

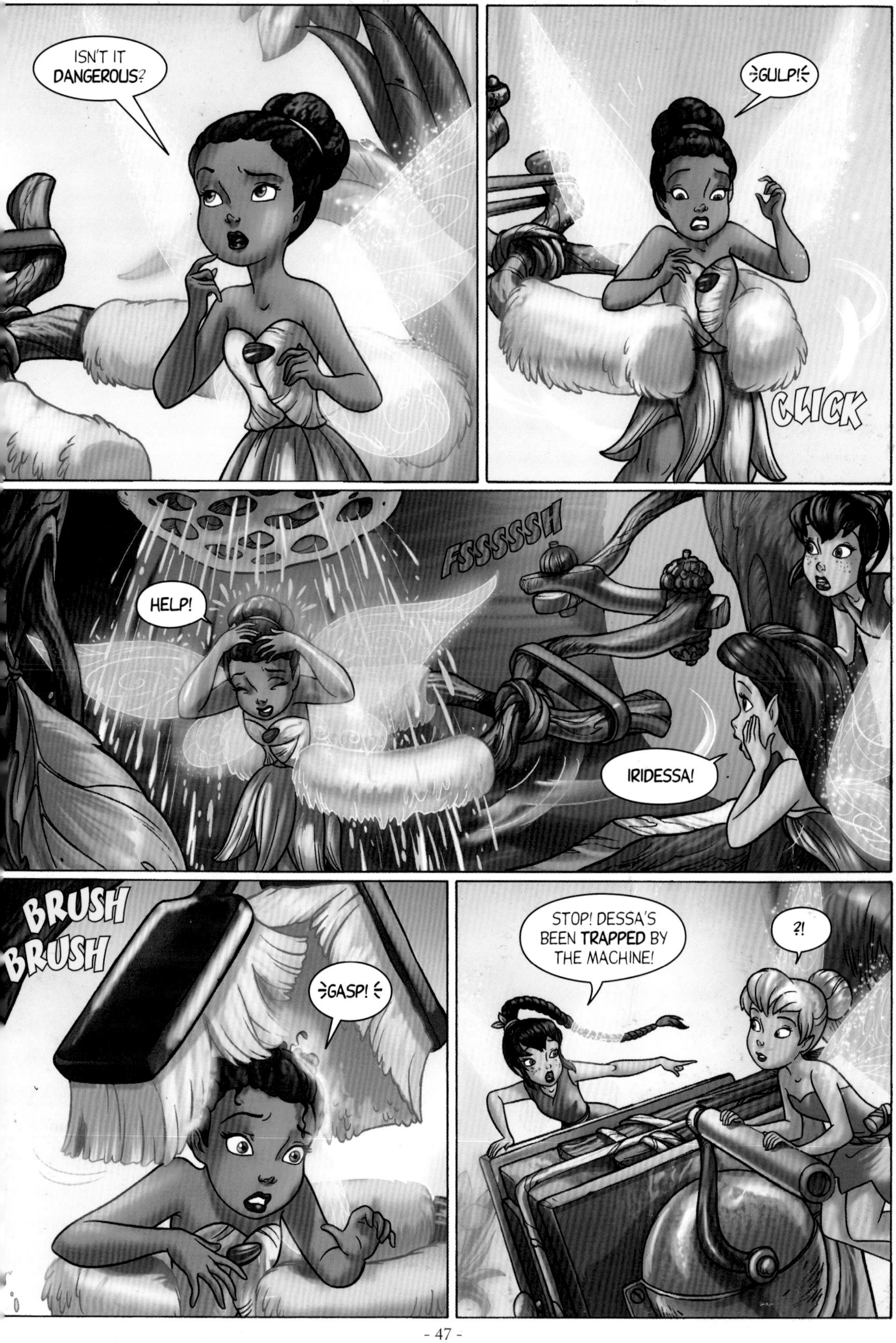

ISN'T IT DANGEROUS?
GULP!
CLICK
FSSSSSH
HELP!
IRIDESSA!
BRUSH
BRUSH
GASP!
STOP! DESSA'S BEEN TRAPPED BY THE MACHINE!
?!

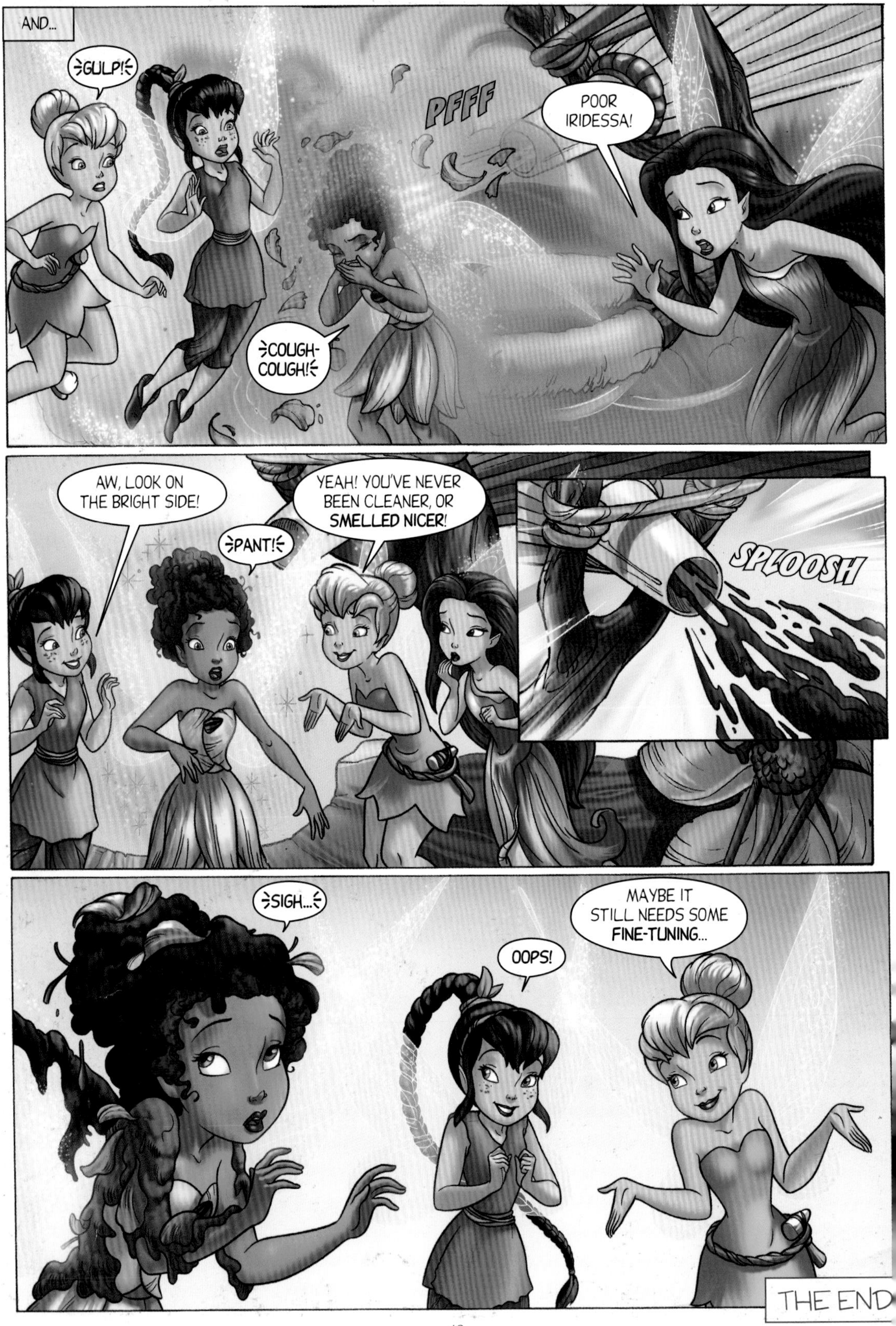
AND...
GULP!
PFFF
POOR IRIDESSA!
COUGH-COUGH!
AW, LOOK ON THE BRIGHT SIDE!
PANT!
YEAH! YOU'VE NEVER BEEN CLEANER, OR **SMELLED NICER**!
SPLOOSH
SIGH...
OOPS!
MAYBE IT STILL NEEDS SOME **FINE-TUNING**...
THE END

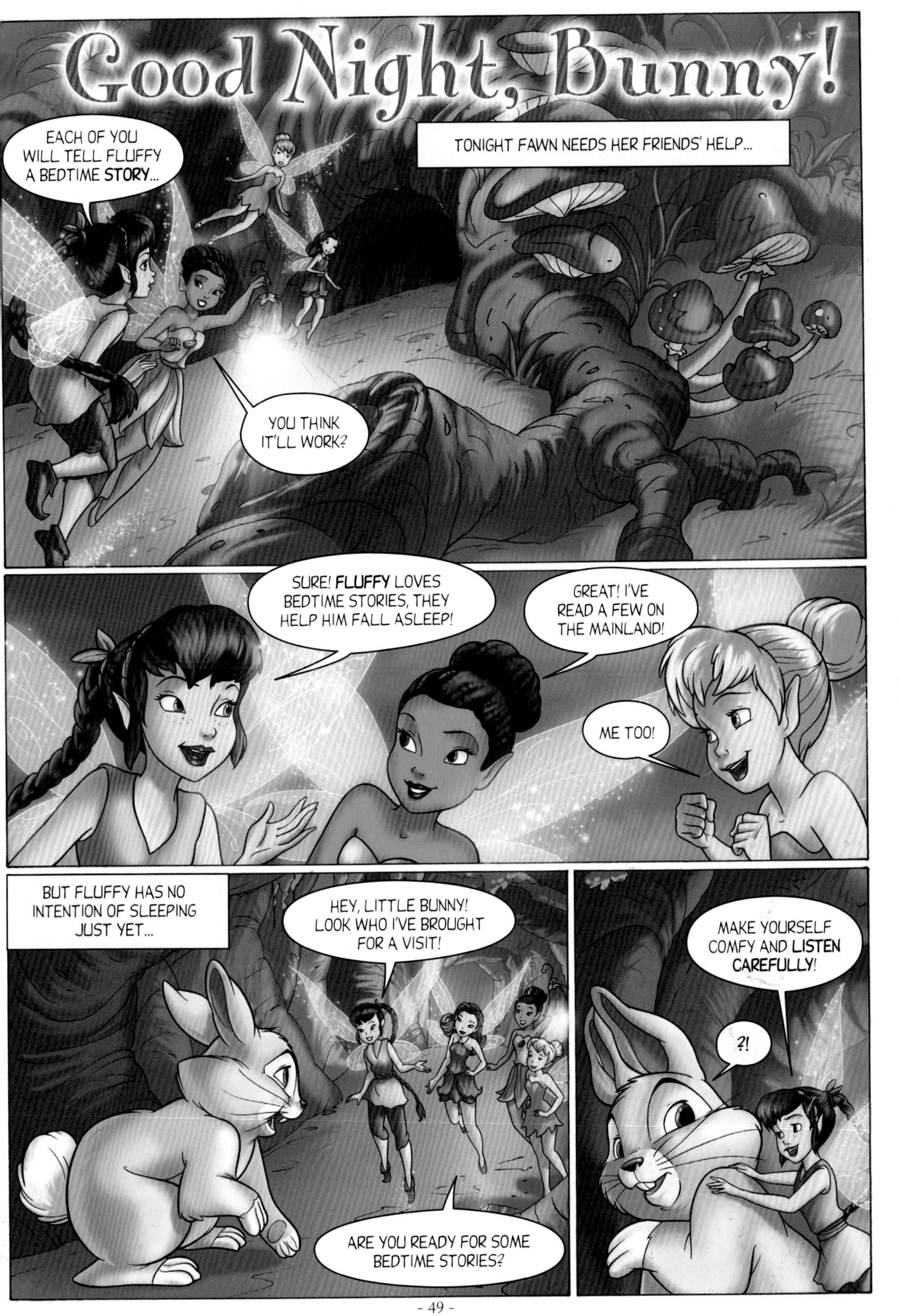
Good Night, Bunny!
TONIGHT FAWN NEEDS HER FRIENDS' HELP...
EACH OF YOU WILL TELL FLUFFY A BEDTIME STORY...
YOU THINK IT'LL WORK?
SURE! FLUFFY LOVES BEDTIME STORIES, THEY HELP HIM FALL ASLEEP!
GREAT! I'VE READ A FEW ON THE MAINLAND!
ME TOO!
BUT FLUFFY HAS NO INTENTION OF SLEEPING JUST YET...
HEY, LITTLE BUNNY! LOOK WHO I'VE BROUGHT FOR A VISIT!
ARE YOU READY FOR SOME BEDTIME STORIES?
MAKE YOURSELF COMFY AND LISTEN CAREFULLY!
?!

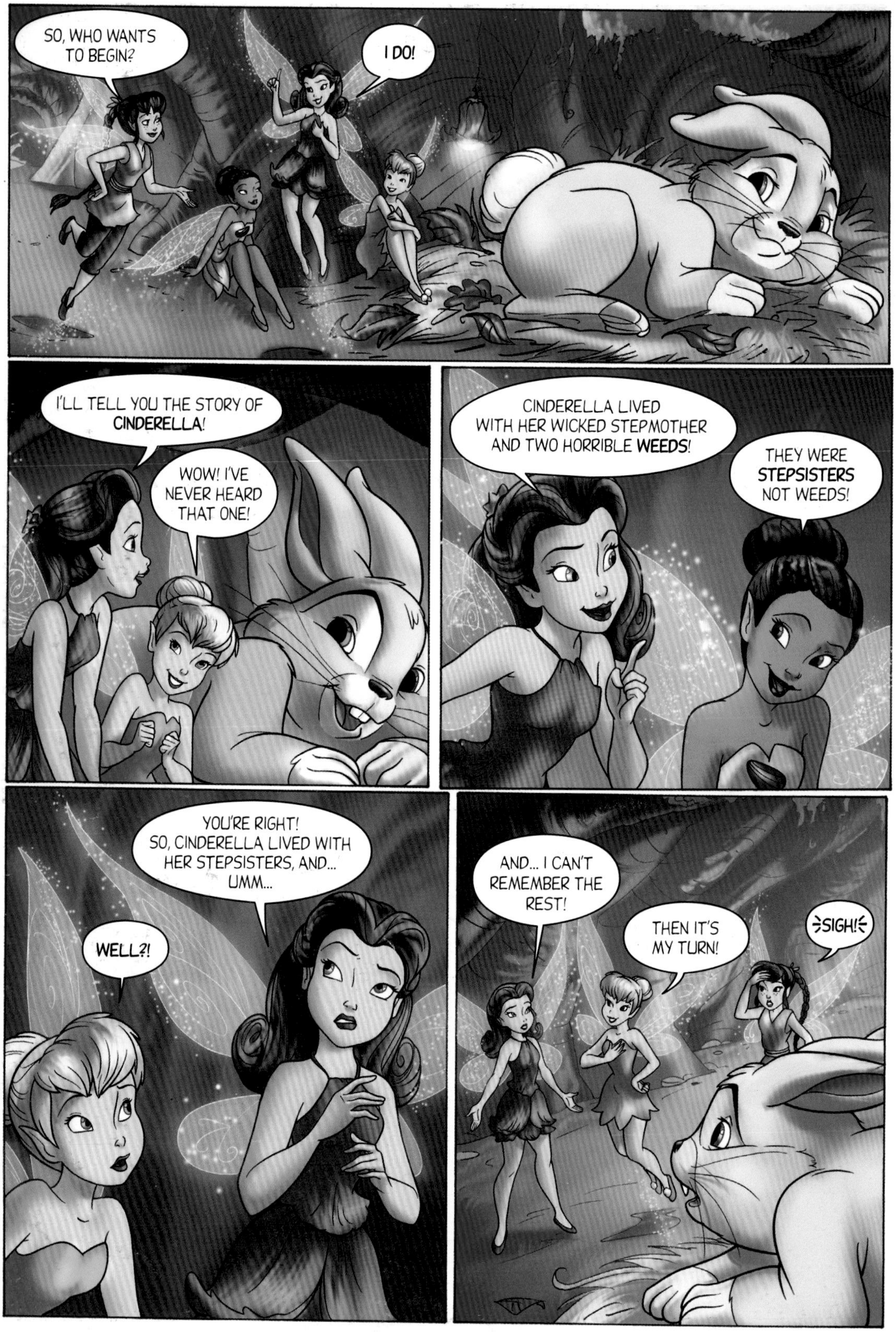
SO, WHO WANTS TO BEGIN?
I DO!
I'LL TELL YOU THE STORY OF CINDERELLA!
WOW! I'VE NEVER HEARD THAT ONE!
CINDERELLA LIVED WITH HER WICKED STEPMOTHER AND TWO HORRIBLE WEEDS!
THEY WERE STEPSISTERS NOT WEEDS!
YOU'RE RIGHT! SO, CINDERELLA LIVED WITH HER STEPSISTERS, AND... UMM...
WELL?!
AND... I CAN'T REMEMBER THE REST!
THEN IT'S MY TURN!
SIGH!

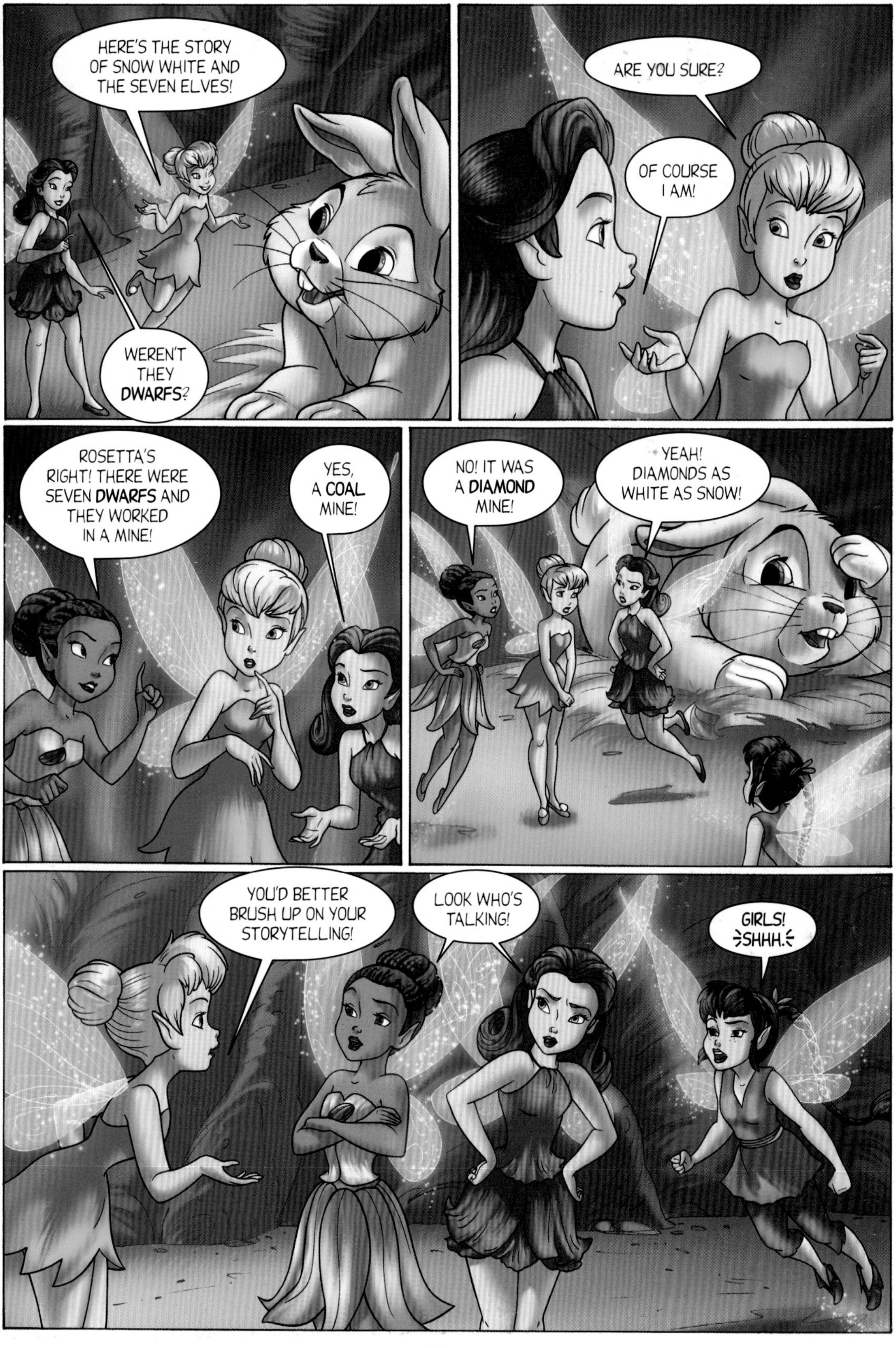
HERE'S THE STORY OF SNOW WHITE AND THE SEVEN ELVES!
WEREN'T THEY **DWARFS**?
ARE YOU SURE?
OF COURSE I AM!
ROSETTA'S RIGHT! THERE WERE SEVEN **DWARFS** AND THEY WORKED IN A MINE!
YES, A **COAL** MINE!
NO! IT WAS A **DIAMOND** MINE!
YEAH! DIAMONDS AS WHITE AS SNOW!
YOU'D BETTER BRUSH UP ON YOUR STORYTELLING!
LOOK WHO'S TALKING!
**GIRLS! SHHH.**

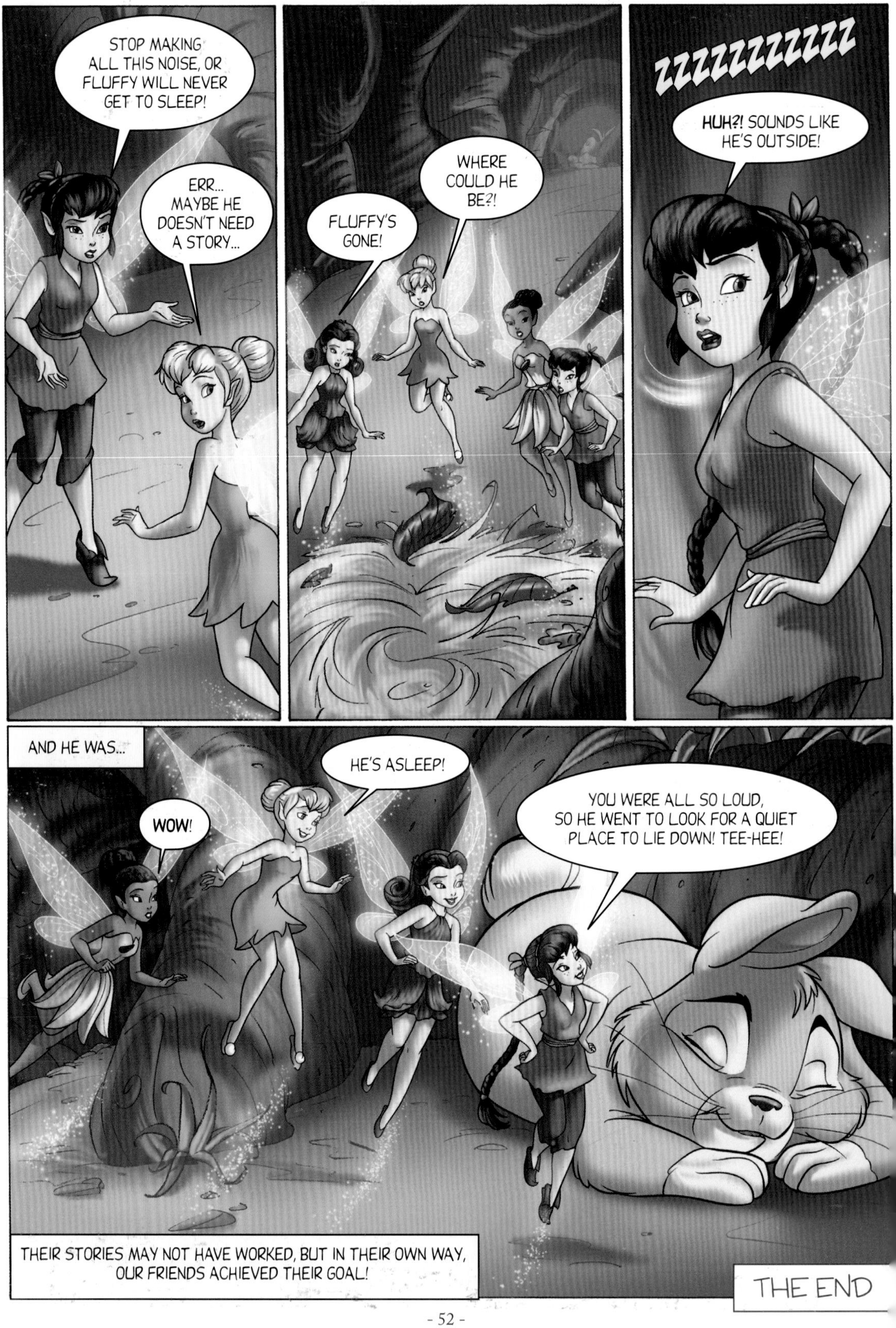

STOP MAKING ALL THIS NOISE, OR FLUFFY WILL NEVER GET TO SLEEP!
ERR... MAYBE HE DOESN'T NEED A STORY...
FLUFFY'S GONE!
WHERE COULD HE BE?!
ZZZZZZZZZZZ
HUH?! SOUNDS LIKE HE'S OUTSIDE!
AND HE WAS...
WOW!
HE'S ASLEEP!
YOU WERE ALL SO LOUD, SO HE WENT TO LOOK FOR A QUIET PLACE TO LIE DOWN! TEE-HEE!
THEIR STORIES MAY NOT HAVE WORKED, BUT IN THEIR OWN WAY, OUR FRIENDS ACHIEVED THEIR GOAL!
THE END

# Cooking Talent?

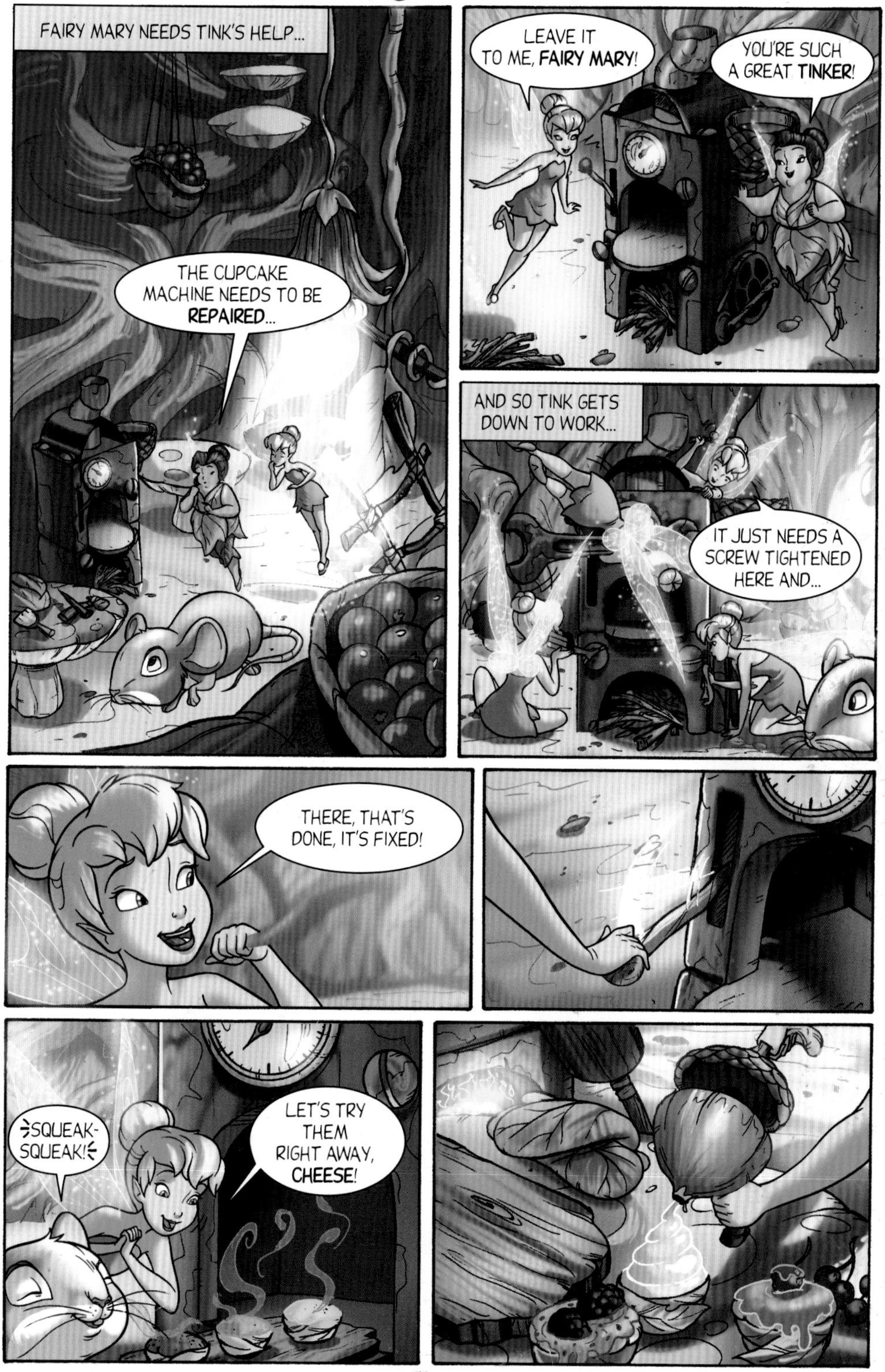
FAIRY MARY NEEDS TINK'S HELP...
THE CUPCAKE MACHINE NEEDS TO BE REPAIRED...
LEAVE IT TO ME, FAIRY MARY!
YOU'RE SUCH A GREAT TINKER!
AND SO TINK GETS DOWN TO WORK...
IT JUST NEEDS A SCREW TIGHTENED HERE AND...
THERE, THAT'S DONE, IT'S FIXED!
SQUEAK-SQUEAK!
LET'S TRY THEM RIGHT AWAY, CHEESE!

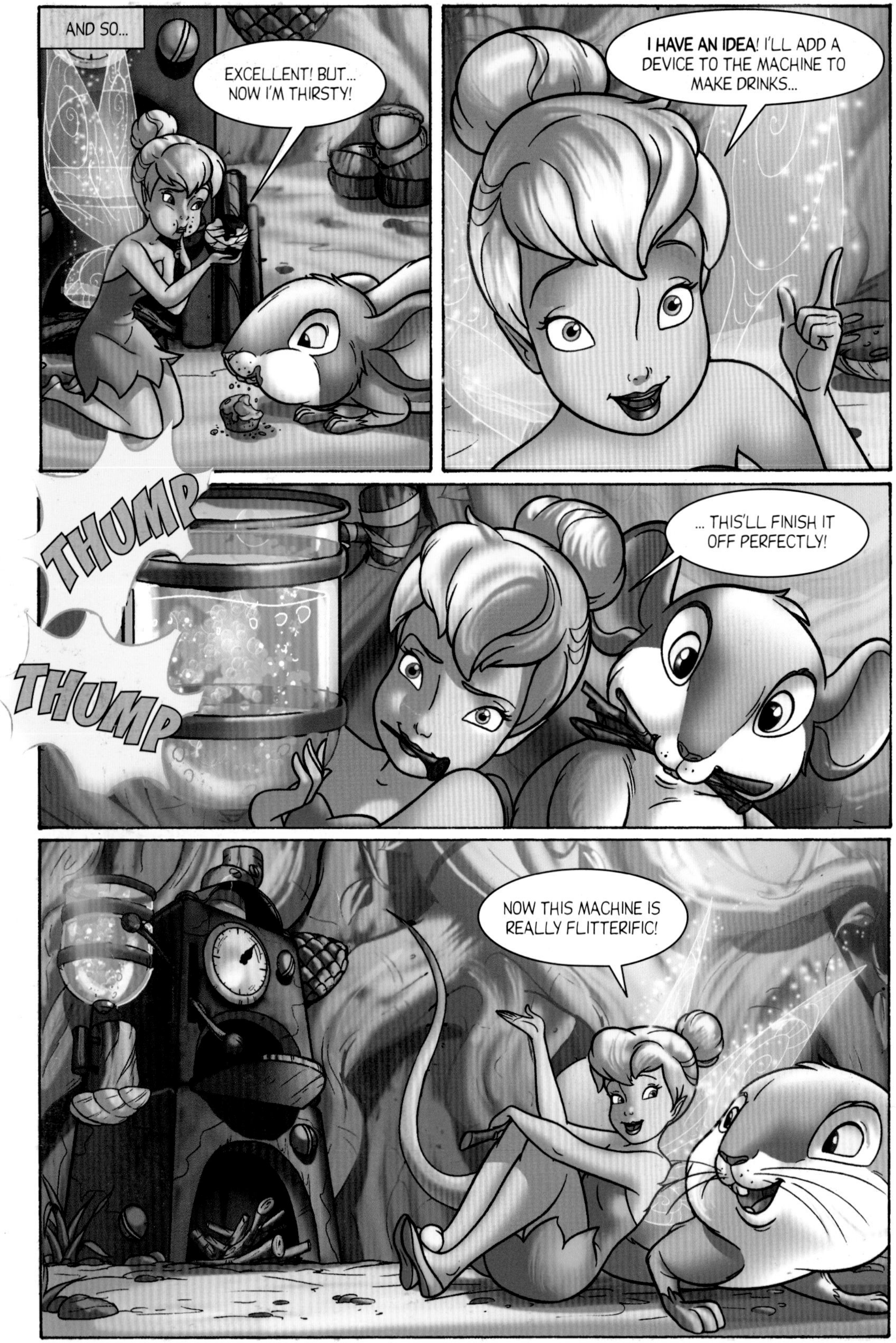
AND SO...
EXCELLENT! BUT... NOW I'M THIRSTY!
I HAVE AN IDEA! I'LL ADD A DEVICE TO THE MACHINE TO MAKE DRINKS...
THUMP
THUMP
... THIS'LL FINISH IT OFF PERFECTLY!
NOW THIS MACHINE IS REALLY FLITTERIFIC!

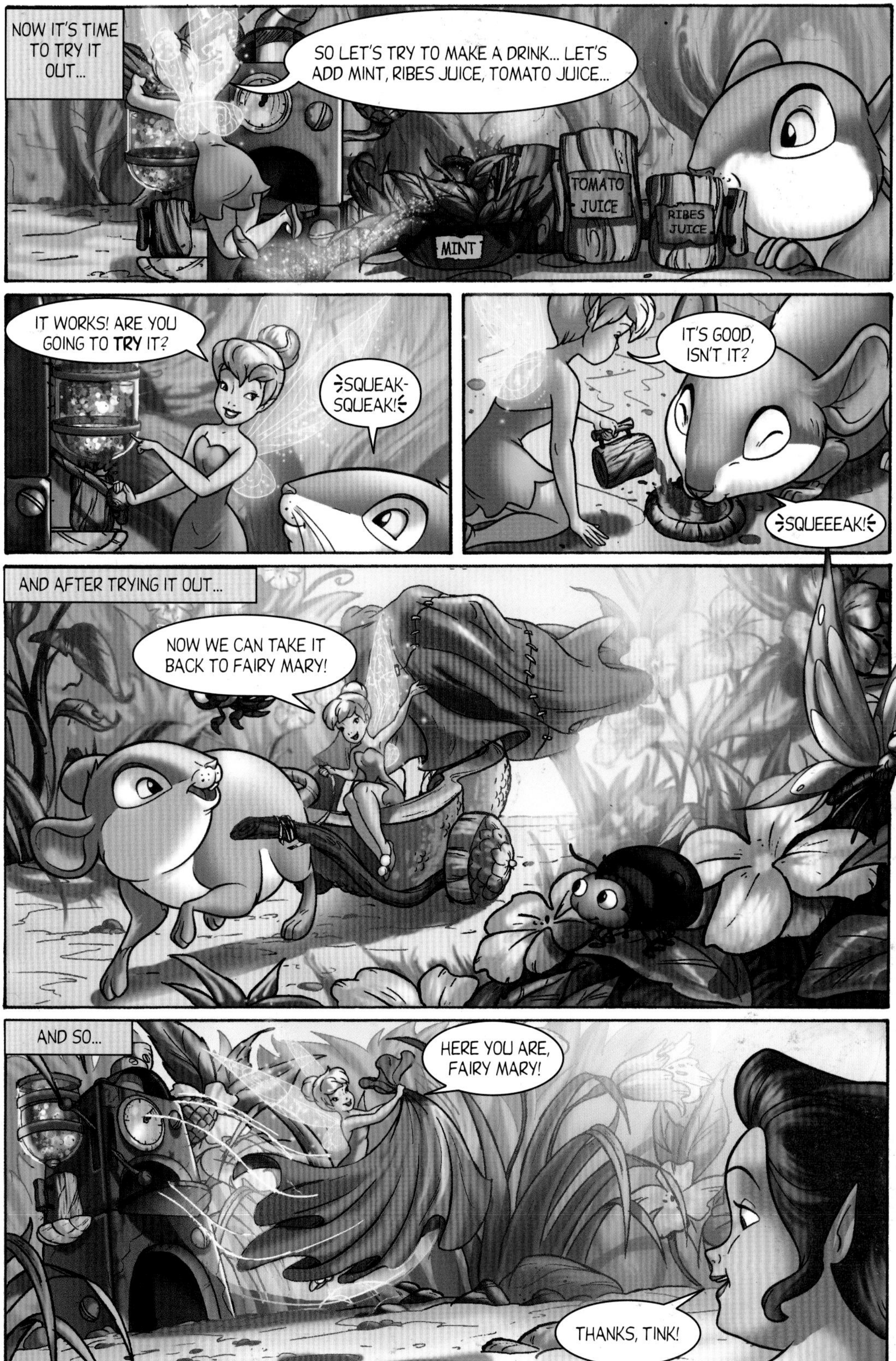
NOW IT'S TIME TO TRY IT OUT...
SO LET'S TRY TO MAKE A DRINK... LET'S ADD MINT, RIBES JUICE, TOMATO JUICE...
TOMATO JUICE
RIBES JUICE
MINT
IT WORKS! ARE YOU GOING TO **TRY** IT?
SQUEAK-SQUEAK!
IT'S GOOD, ISN'T IT?
SQUEEEAK!
AND AFTER TRYING IT OUT...
NOW WE CAN TAKE IT BACK TO FAIRY MARY!
AND SO...
HERE YOU ARE, FAIRY MARY!
THANKS, TINK!

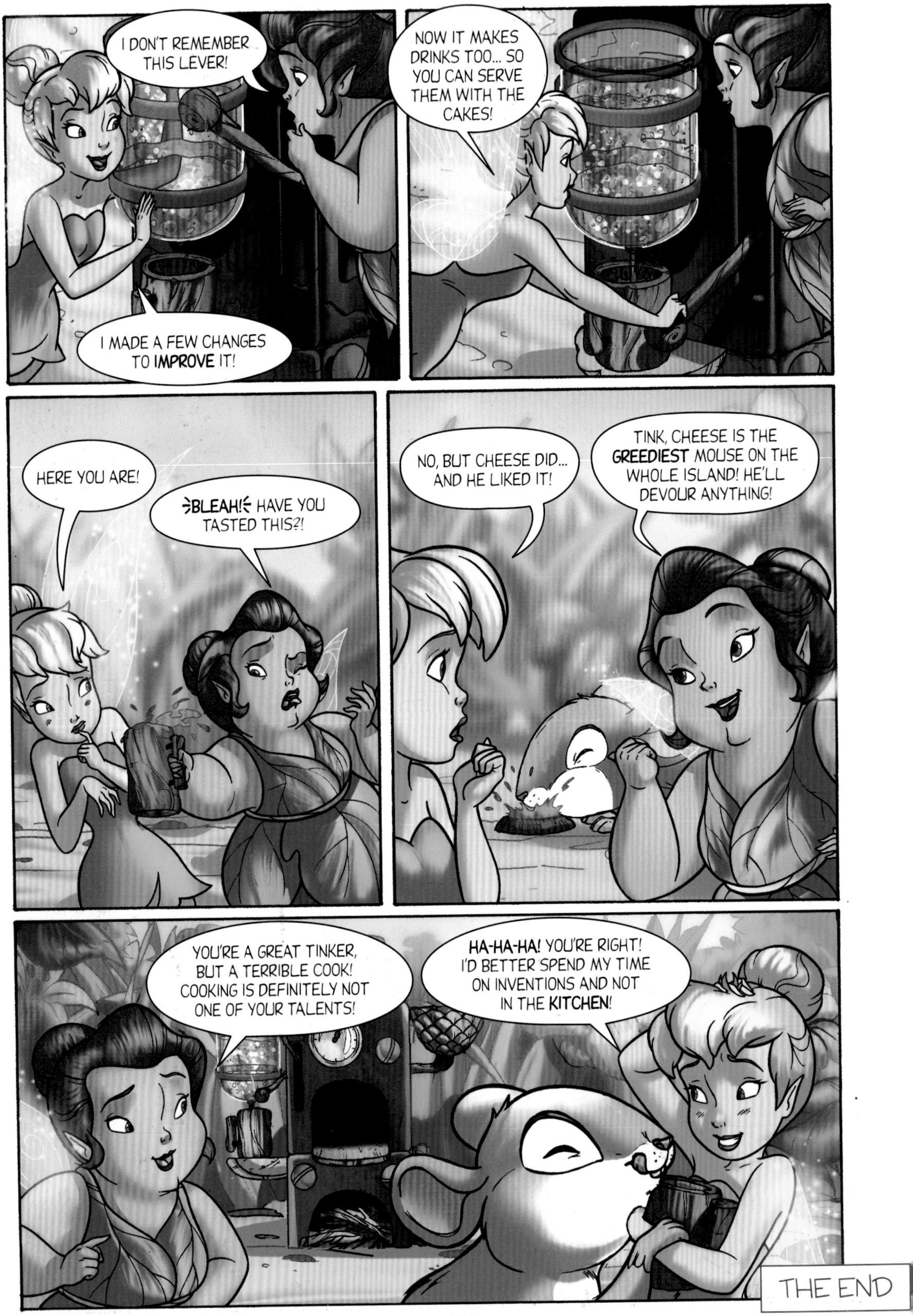
I DON'T REMEMBER THIS LEVER!
I MADE A FEW CHANGES TO **IMPROVE** IT!
NOW IT MAKES DRINKS TOO... SO YOU CAN SERVE THEM WITH THE CAKES!
HERE YOU ARE!
BLEAH! HAVE YOU TASTED THIS?!
NO, BUT CHEESE DID... AND HE LIKED IT!
TINK, CHEESE IS THE **GREEDIEST** MOUSE ON THE WHOLE ISLAND! HE'LL DEVOUR ANYTHING!
YOU'RE A GREAT TINKER, BUT A TERRIBLE COOK! COOKING IS DEFINITELY NOT ONE OF YOUR TALENTS!
**HA-HA-HA!** YOU'RE RIGHT! I'D BETTER SPEND MY TIME ON INVENTIONS AND NOT IN THE **KITCHEN**!
THE END

# A Little Nap

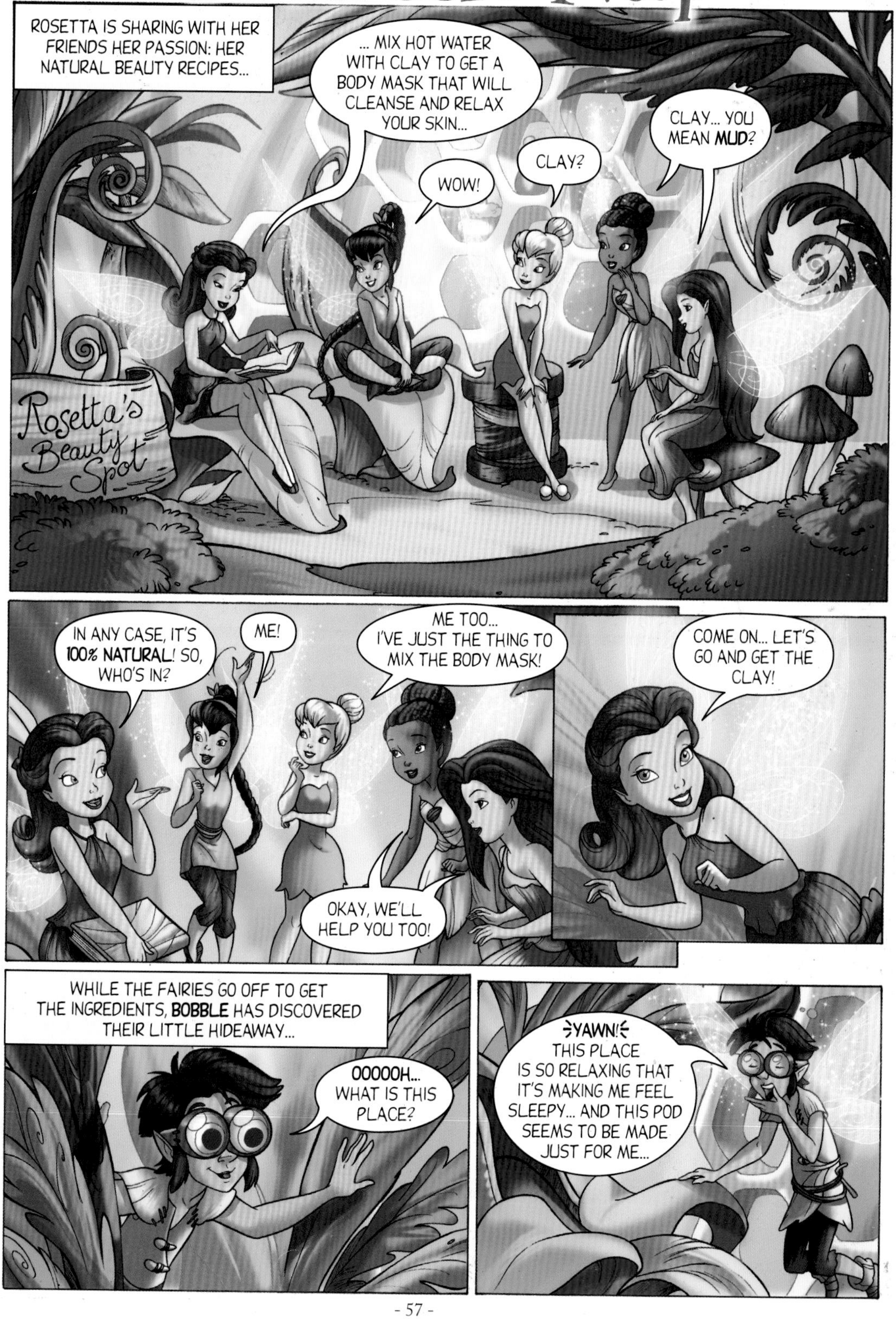

ROSETTA IS SHARING WITH HER FRIENDS HER PASSION: HER NATURAL BEAUTY RECIPES...
... MIX HOT WATER WITH CLAY TO GET A BODY MASK THAT WILL CLEANSE AND RELAX YOUR SKIN...
WOW!
CLAY?
CLAY... YOU MEAN **MUD**?
Rosetta's Beauty Spot
IN ANY CASE, IT'S **100% NATURAL**! SO, WHO'S IN?
ME!
ME TOO... I'VE JUST THE THING TO MIX THE BODY MASK!
OKAY, WE'LL HELP YOU TOO!
COME ON... LET'S GO AND GET THE CLAY!
WHILE THE FAIRIES GO OFF TO GET THE INGREDIENTS, **BOBBLE** HAS DISCOVERED THEIR LITTLE HIDEAWAY...
**OOOOOH...** WHAT IS THIS PLACE?
**YAWN!** THIS PLACE IS SO RELAXING THAT IT'S MAKING ME FEEL SLEEPY... AND THIS POD SEEMS TO BE MADE JUST FOR ME...

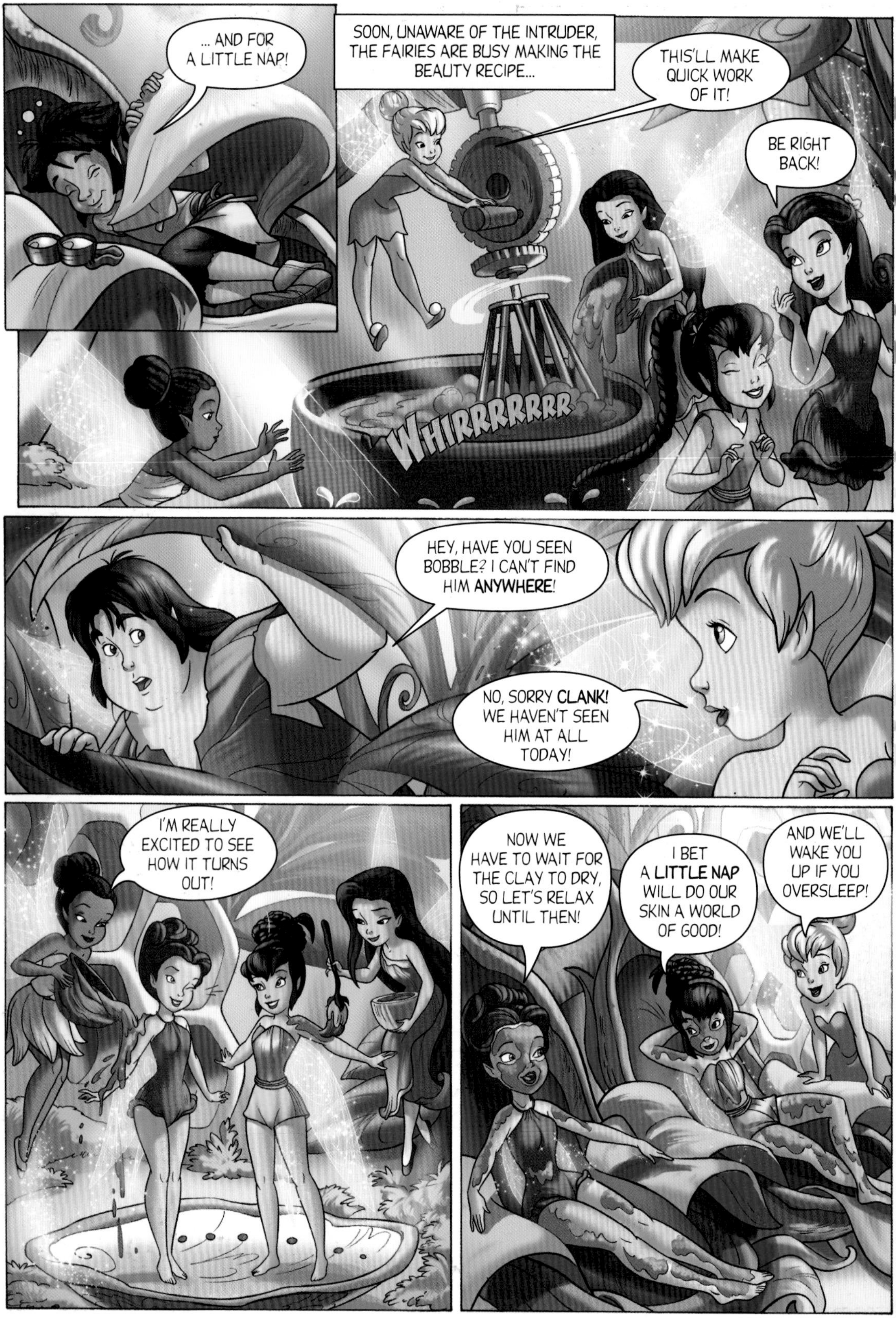
... AND FOR A LITTLE NAP!
SOON, UNAWARE OF THE INTRUDER, THE FAIRIES ARE BUSY MAKING THE BEAUTY RECIPE...
THIS'LL MAKE QUICK WORK OF IT!
BE RIGHT BACK!
WHIRRRRRRR
HEY, HAVE YOU SEEN BOBBLE? I CAN'T FIND HIM ANYWHERE!
NO, SORRY CLANK! WE HAVEN'T SEEN HIM AT ALL TODAY!
I'M REALLY EXCITED TO SEE HOW IT TURNS OUT!
NOW WE HAVE TO WAIT FOR THE CLAY TO DRY, SO LET'S RELAX UNTIL THEN!
I BET A LITTLE NAP WILL DO OUR SKIN A WORLD OF GOOD!
AND WE'LL WAKE YOU UP IF YOU OVERSLEEP!

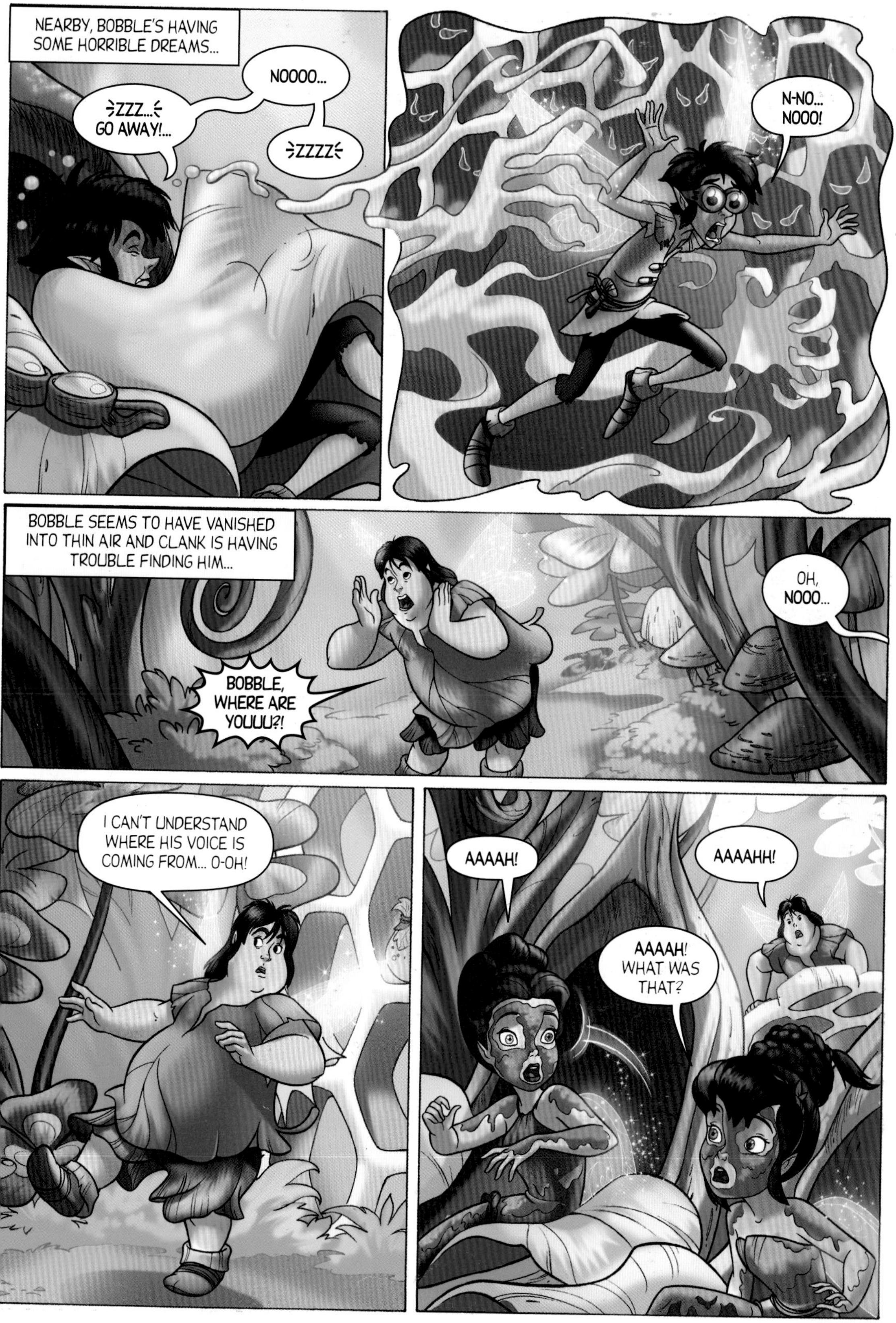
NEARBY, BOBBLE'S HAVING SOME HORRIBLE DREAMS...
ZZZ... GO AWAY!...
NOOOO...
ZZZZ
N-NO... NOOO!
BOBBLE SEEMS TO HAVE VANISHED INTO THIN AIR AND CLANK IS HAVING TROUBLE FINDING HIM...
BOBBLE, WHERE ARE YOUUU?!
OH, NOOO...
I CAN'T UNDERSTAND WHERE HIS VOICE IS COMING FROM... O-OH!
AAAAH!
AAAAHH!
AAAAH! WHAT WAS THAT?

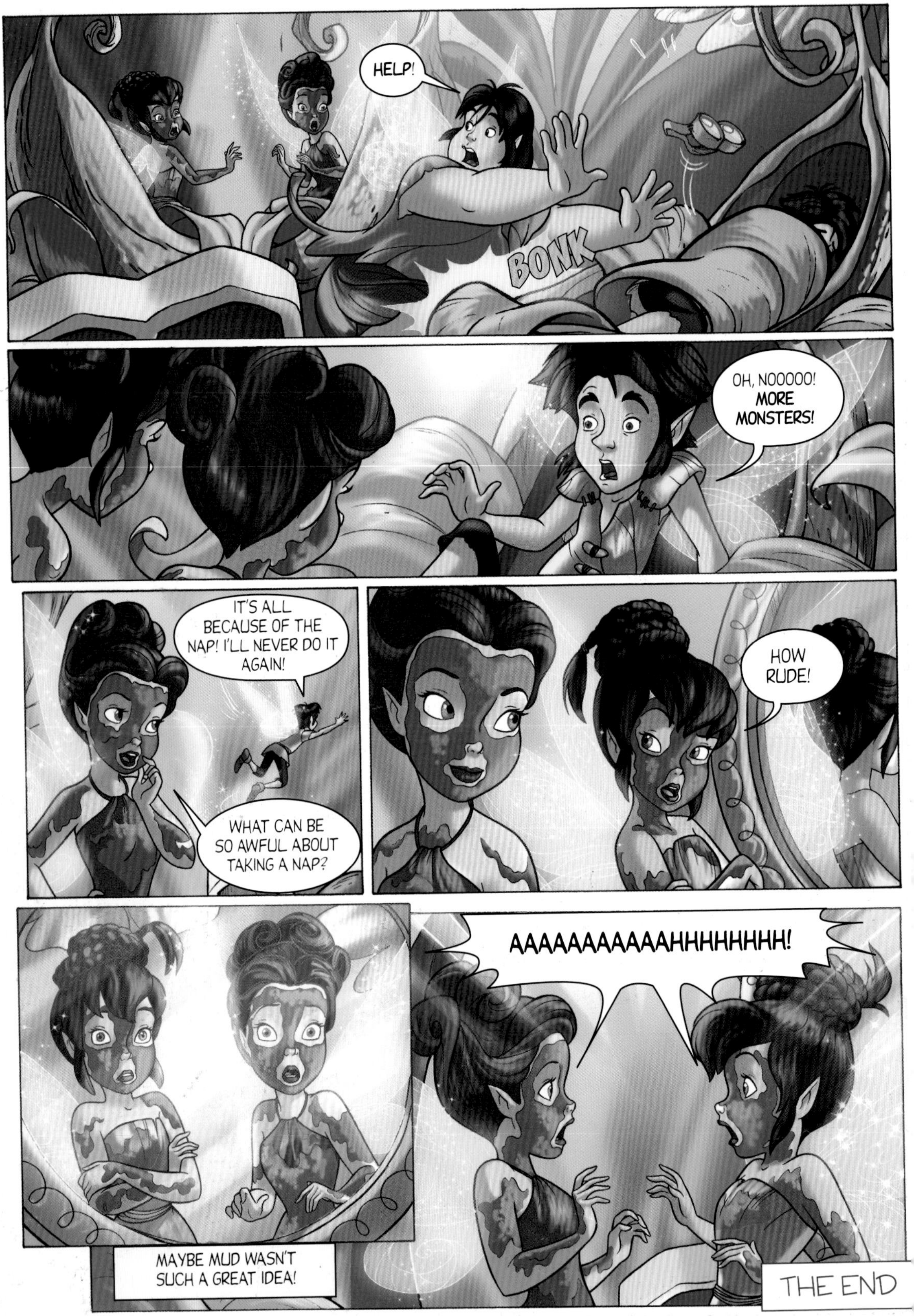
HELP!
BONK
OH, NOOOOO! MORE MONSTERS!
IT'S ALL BECAUSE OF THE NAP! I'LL NEVER DO IT AGAIN!
WHAT CAN BE SO AWFUL ABOUT TAKING A NAP?
HOW RUDE!
AAAAAAAAAAAHHHHHHHH!
MAYBE MUD WASN'T SUCH A GREAT IDEA!
THE END

# WATCH OUT FOR PAPERCUTZ™

Welcome to the totally Tinker Bell-filled (Well, except for a couple of stories!) twentieth DISNEY FAIRIES graphic novel from Papercutz—those not-too secretive folks dedicated to publishing great graphic novels for all ages! I'm Jim Salicrup, the Editor-in-Chief and honorary member of The Lost Boys, and I'm here to take a few moments to look back and celebrate our twentieth DISNEY FAIRIES graphic novel...

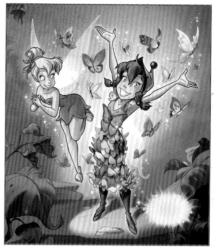

If you were one of the lucky ones who picked up the very first printing of DISNEY FAIRIES #1, you would've seen one of our most embarrassing boo-boos—we accidentally featured Beck on the front cover instead of Prilla! DISNEY FAIRIES #1 was titled "Prilla's Talent," and it did indeed feature a story called "Prilla's Talent," which was all about that particular fairy's unique talent. What DISNEY FAIRIES #1 did not include was a story called "The Most Beautiful Dress," the story that featured the fairy called Beck. That story was published in DISNEY FAIRIES #2 "Tinker Bell and the Wings of Rani." Oopsie!

But fortunately, one of the wonderful things about graphic novel publishing, and book publishing in general, is that when a book sells out of its print run, if there's still enough demand for the book, it'll go back to press, and that provides the opportunity for publishers to correct any mistakes that may've slipped by in the previous printings. DISNEY FAIRIES #1 sold out quickly and eventually we replaced the original cover of DISNEY FAIRIES #1 with the current cover, which shows Tinker Bell kinda shushing you. Guess she doesn't want anyone to notice that Prilla's still not on the cover! Hey, as revealed in DISNEY FAIRIES #1, page 12, panel 1, the fairies call us humans "Clumsies"! I guess now we know why! And if you're wondering exactly what is Prilla's talent, I'm happy to inform you that all twenty DISNEY FAIRIES graphic novels are still available at booksellers everywhere, and at all the very best libraries. Another bit of DISNEY FAIRIES lore was also revealed in DISNEY FAIRIES #1—that the fairies never say they're sorry. Instead they say "I'd fly backward if I could." So, at this very late date, I hope you'll allow this humble "Clumsy" to offer a sincere "I'd fly backward if I could"!

While we're talking about the DISNEY FAIRIES graphic novels, here's a quick trivia question to test your knowledge regarding the special history of this graphic novel series: How many DISNEY FAIRIES graphic novels has Papercutz published? If you answered 20, you're close! But the correct answer is 21! In addition to the twenty DISNEY FAIRIES graphic novels in this series, we also published a graphic novel adaptation of ***Tinker Bell and the Great Fairy Rescue*** as a separate title. But that wasn't the only Tinker Bell movie adaptation we published...

DISNEY FAIRIES #12 featured "Tinker Bell and the Lost Treasure," #13 adapted "Tinker Bell and the Pixie Hollow Games," #15 brought us "Tinker Bell and the Secret of the Wings," #16 included "Tinker Bell and the Pirate Fairy," and finally, #17 told the story of "Tinker Bell and the NeverBeast'"! Each of these graphic novels make perfect companions to the Tinker Bell Disney DVDs!

Disney
MINNIE & DAISY
BEST FRIENDS FOREVER
FASHION PASSION
Disney COMICS
PAPERCUTZ

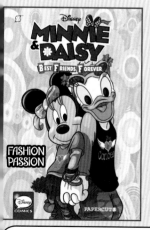

DISNEY FAIRIES was the first DISNEY GRAPHIC NOVEL series published by Papercutz, and we're happy to say we've since added the following Disney series to the Papercutz line-up of great graphic novels:

**X-MICKEY** – Join Mickey Mouse as he explores all sorts of spooky supernatural mysteries!

**DISNEY PARODIES** – Imagine great works of literature or the most popular movies of all time spoofed and recast with all your favorite Disney stars! The first volume featured "Mickey's Inferno," a satirical retelling of Dante's *Divine Comedy*! Volume Two kicks into warp drive and spoofs *Star Wars* in "Planetary Wars."

**MINNIE & DAISY** – Fun-filled High School hi-jinks starring Minnie Mouse and Daisy Duck and their friends. Check out the preview of MINNIE & DAISY #2 "Fashion Passion" on the pages following!

**THE ZODIAC LEGACY** – An all-new team of super-powered teenagers, created by Stan Lee, the co-creator of *Spider-Man*, *Iron Man*, *Thor*, *Dr. Strange*, and many more!

## STAY IN TOUCH!

EMAIL: salicrup@papercutz.com
WEB: papercutz.com
TWITTER: @papercutzgn
FACEBOOK: PAPERCUTZGRAPHICNOVELS
REGULAR MAIL: Papercutz, 160 Broadway, Suite 700, East Wing, New York, NY 10038

And that's not all! Coming soon from Papercutz is an all-new line of graphic novels for girls called Charmz, and one of the graphic novel series included in that line is an all-new series created by Disney! What is it? Check out papercutz.com for the full story! In the meantime, there are plenty of other DISNEY GRAPHIC NOVELS available to keep you busy, so keep on believing in "faith, trust, and pixie dust"!

Thanks, Jim

SPECIAL PREVIEW of MINNIE & DAISY #2 "Fashion Passion!" ...

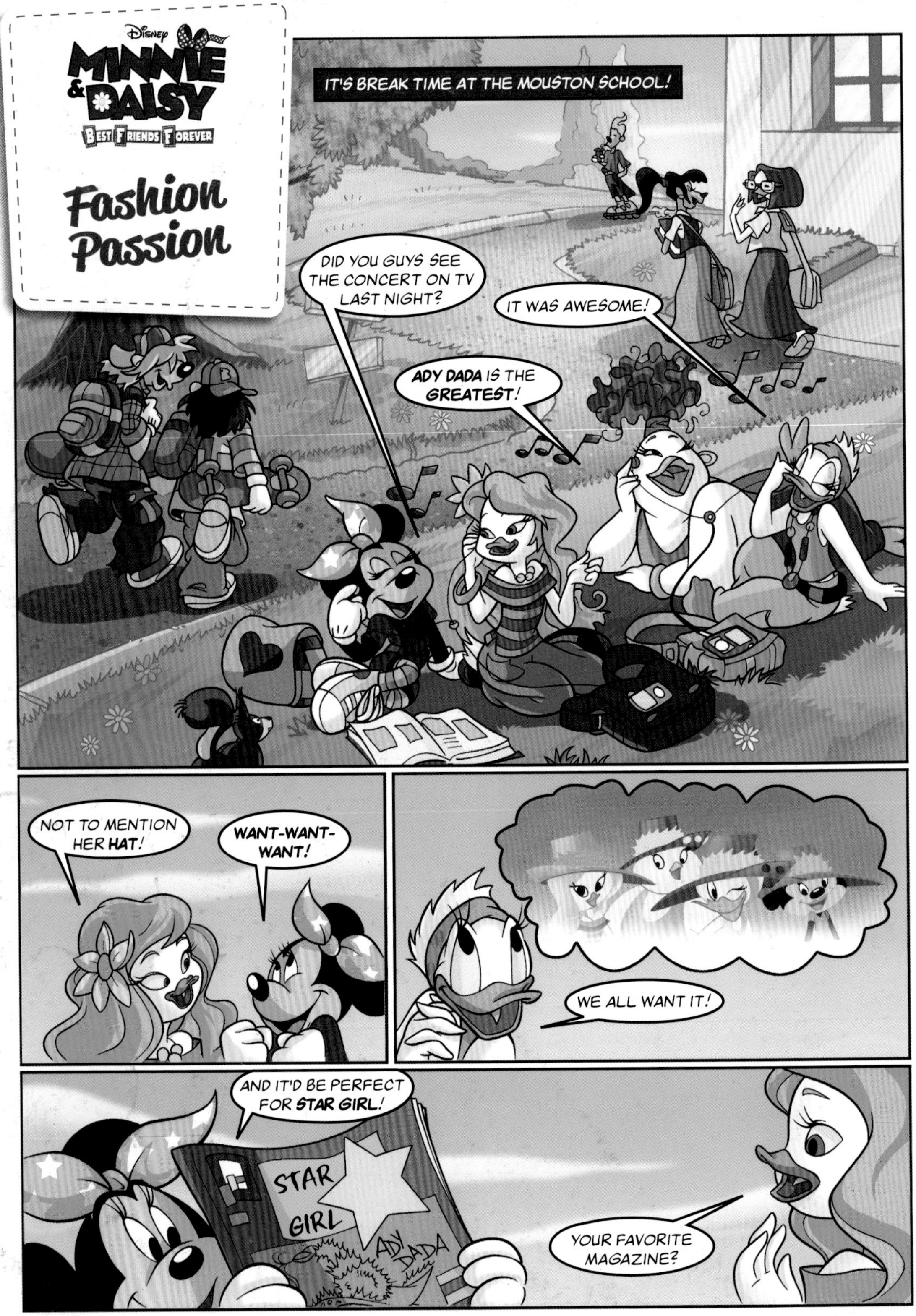
Disney
MINNIE & DAISY
BEST FRIENDS FOREVER
Fashion Passion
IT'S BREAK TIME AT THE MOUSTON SCHOOL!
DID YOU GUYS SEE THE CONCERT ON TV LAST NIGHT?
IT WAS AWESOME!
ADY DADA IS THE GREATEST!
NOT TO MENTION HER HAT!
WANT-WANT-WANT!
WE ALL WANT IT!
AND IT'D BE PERFECT FOR STAR GIRL!
STAR GIRL
ADY DADA
YOUR FAVORITE MAGAZINE?

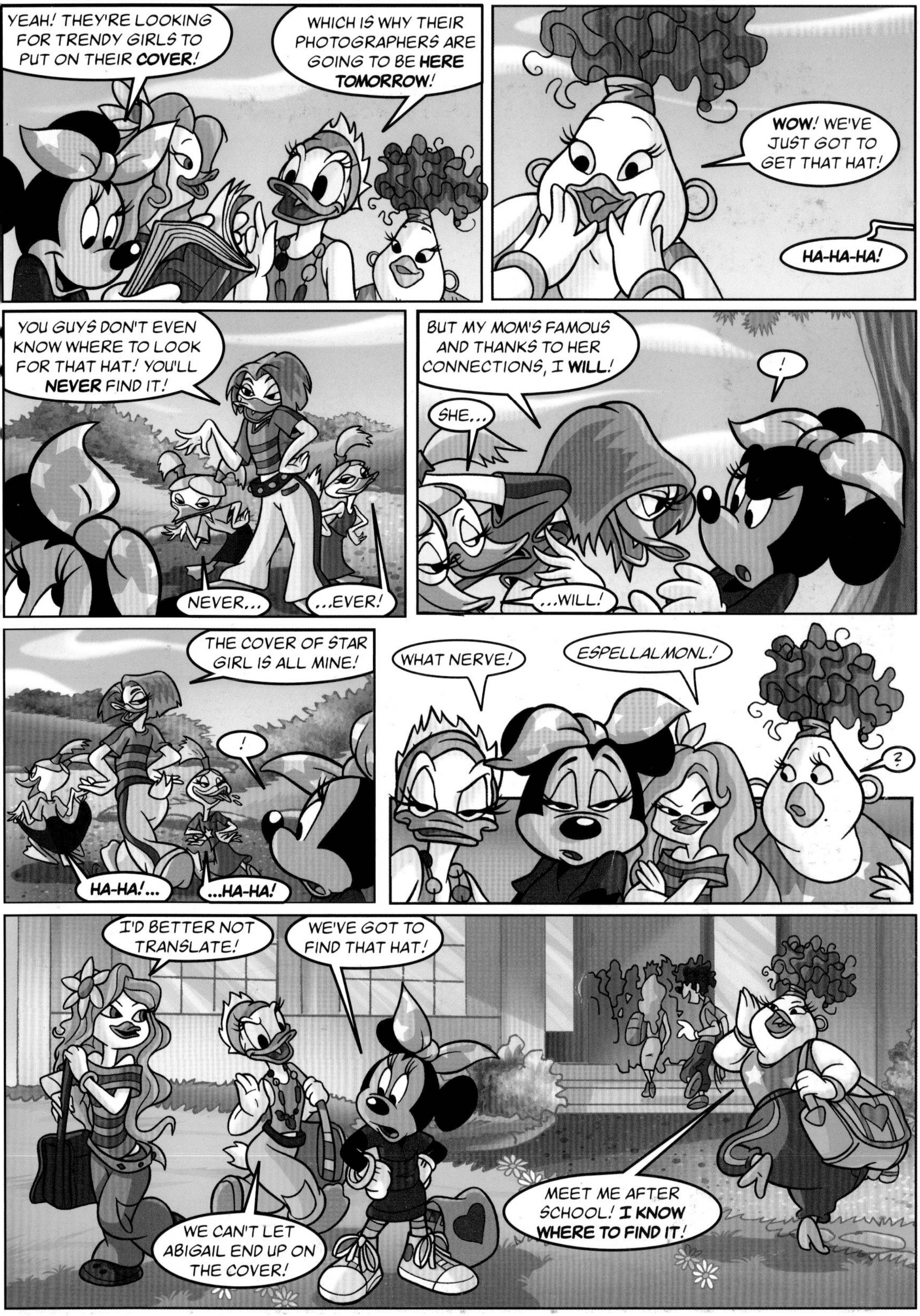
YEAH! THEY'RE LOOKING FOR TRENDY GIRLS TO PUT ON THEIR COVER!
WHICH IS WHY THEIR PHOTOGRAPHERS ARE GOING TO BE HERE TOMORROW!
WOW! WE'VE JUST GOT TO GET THAT HAT!
HA-HA-HA!
YOU GUYS DON'T EVEN KNOW WHERE TO LOOK FOR THAT HAT! YOU'LL NEVER FIND IT!
NEVER...
...EVER!
BUT MY MOM'S FAMOUS AND THANKS TO HER CONNECTIONS, I WILL!
SHE...
...WILL!
!
THE COVER OF STAR GIRL IS ALL MINE!
!
HA-HA!...
...HA-HA!
WHAT NERVE!
ESPELLALMONL!
?
I'D BETTER NOT TRANSLATE!
WE'VE GOT TO FIND THAT HAT!
WE CAN'T LET ABIGAIL END UP ON THE COVER!
MEET ME AFTER SCHOOL! I KNOW WHERE TO FIND IT!

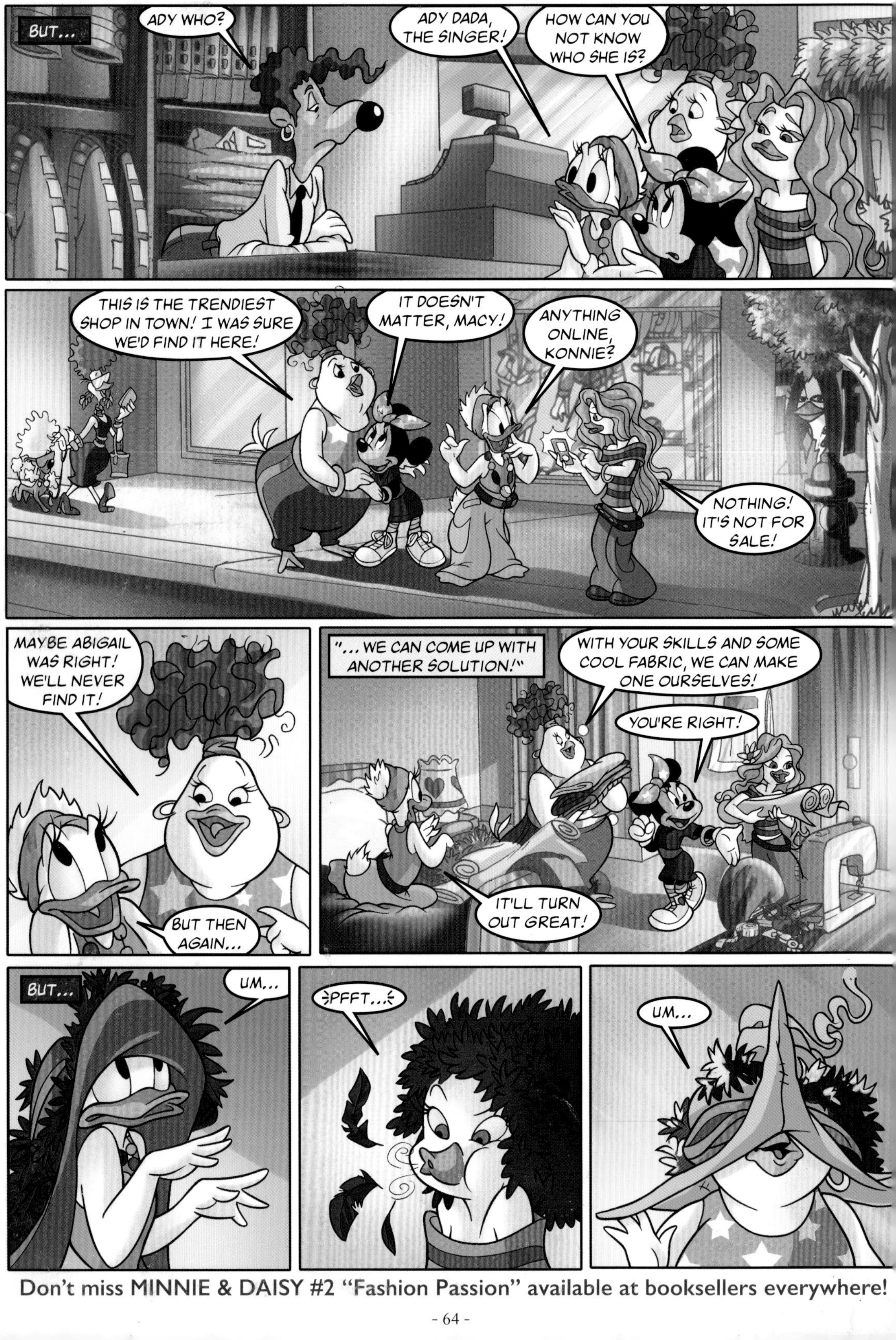
BUT...
ADY WHO?
ADY DADA, THE SINGER!
HOW CAN YOU NOT KNOW WHO SHE IS?
THIS IS THE TRENDIEST SHOP IN TOWN! I WAS SURE WE'D FIND IT HERE!
IT DOESN'T MATTER, MACY!
ANYTHING ONLINE, KONNIE?
NOTHING! IT'S NOT FOR SALE!
MAYBE ABIGAIL WAS RIGHT! WE'LL NEVER FIND IT!
BUT THEN AGAIN...
"...WE CAN COME UP WITH ANOTHER SOLUTION!"
WITH YOUR SKILLS AND SOME COOL FABRIC, WE CAN MAKE ONE OURSELVES!
YOU'RE RIGHT!
IT'LL TURN OUT GREAT!
BUT...
UM...
PFFT...
UM...

Don't miss MINNIE & DAISY #2 "Fashion Passion" available at booksellers everywhere!